JOURNEY OUTSIDE
Mary Q. Steele
Newbery Honor Book

They were headed for the Better Place, Grandfather said, although he could remember nothing about it except the words "green" and "day." But Dilar suspected that they were headed nowhere, simply following the dark underground river blindly, going in circles. And so one night, on impulse, he leaped onto a shelf of rock and watched the flotilla of the Raft People disappear into the darkness.

If he was right, Dilar reasoned, the rafts would soon come again. But he hadn't known about the rats waiting among the rocks. In terror and desperation he flung himself up a tall, narrow crevice, climbing frantically, until suddenly he found himself in a different world, a world so beautiful and strange he could only suppose he had died—a world of day, and sun, and trees, and sky.

Fast-paced, filled with action and excitement, *Journey Outside* is much more than an adventure. It is also a wholly contemporary story of a search for real answers in a bewildering and strange world that is often as terrifying as it is beautiful.

MARY Q. STEELE

JOURNEY OUTSIDE

PUFFIN BOOKS

For Allerton, who taught me much of what is in this book

". . . Now I confess that the world, more beautiful
for your presence, was not fine enough to warrant
my summoning you into it . . ."

The three lines of poetry included in the dedication are taken from the poem
"Forgive Me" by Dilys Laing, and are reprinted by permission of Alexander Laing.

PUFFIN BOOKS
Published by the Penguin Group
Penguin Books USA Inc., 375 Hudson Street, New York, New York 10014, U.S.A.
Penguin Books Ltd, 27 Wrights Lane, London W8 5TZ, England
Penguin Books Australia Ltd, Ringwood, Victoria, Australia
Penguin Books Canada Ltd, 10 Alcorn Avenue, Toronto, Ontario, Canada M4V 3B2
Penguin Books (N.Z.) Ltd, 182–190 Wairau Road, Auckland 10, New Zealand

Penguin Books Ltd, Registered Offices: Harmondsworth, Middlesex, England

First published by The Viking Press 1969
Published in Puffin Books 1979

19 20

Library of Congress Cataloging in Publication Data
Steele, Mary Q. Journey Outside.
Summary: The Raft People live in darkness and travel a circular journey
on an underground river. One boy finds his way outside and tries to learn
as much as possible so he can utlimately lead his people to the Better Place.
[1. Fantasy] I. Title. PZ7.S8146Jo 1979 [Fic] 79-9919
ISBN 0 14 03.0588 2

Printed in the United States of America

CHAPTER 1

"Watch out, Grandfather!"

The old man dropped his fishbone spoon, covered his face with his hands, and cowered against the floor of the raft. Dilar sped by, the wind from his passing made the stewpot rock unsteadily, and then he dove off the end of the raft, sending a shower of drops hissing into the fire.

Grandfather scrambled up and retrieved his spoon. "Be careful, Dilar," he shouted. "There are willimars about. I saw one this morning!"

Dilar did not answer. He swam on until he reached the next raft, and hauled himself aboard. He got to his feet and ran again. It was one of the long rafts, holding four families, and it almost gave him a chance to reach some speed. One of the women looked up and smiled as he flashed by, but most of the others, if they noticed him at all, frowned and shook their heads.

Once again he went headlong into the water and swam as fast as he could, out of the light of the flickering fish-oil torches and into the dim interval between the rafts. It was never truly dark, for though the feeble shine from the rafts rapidly faded, the water seemed to catch and reflect light from a thousand sources and there was always a faint radiance over the river.

In a few minutes he caught sight of the gleam of the torches on Bimar's raft, ahead of him. He swam a little faster and in ten strokes could lay his hand on the edge of the raft. He did not pull himself onto it, however. There was no need. Even at this distance he could tell that Bimar's father was in one of his black moods and that Bimar would not be able to join him in any kind of game this time.

Bimar, who was helping his father haul in a net full of fish, glanced around at Dilar. He looked unhappy. His sister was standing nearby, ready to help sort the fish into piles, those for immediate eating, those for drying, and the ones that her mother and younger brother would put between two stones and press to extract the oil. She held a knife for skinning the larger ones.

Dilar watched them. He wondered how it would be to have a mother, a brother, and a sister. His own mother had died so long ago he could no longer remember her. His father and grandfather were all the family he'd ever had.

Of course, of all the Raft People only Bimar's mother and father had three children. Most families had two, and some had only one or none at all. There would come a time soon, Dilar's father often said, when there would only be twenty-two rafts instead of twenty-three. And then perhaps twenty-one. And then twenty?

Dilar gave a little shiver. Perhaps this was what put Bimar's father into his dark tempers so often lately. Dilar himself had spells when he was uneasy, when the rafts and the river and the rock-lined waterways and the fish-oil torches all seemed to him to be one gray, threatening menace he did not understand, or when living seemed blank and pointless. He hated these times. It wasn't the way things were supposed to be.

He saw Bimar glance at him again and he made a sympathetic face and slipped down into the water. He pushed himself away from the raft and swam slowly against the gentle current.

Mostly he could get rid of fears and depressions by playing games, by running and swimming very fast, the whole length of the flotilla. In fact he had not this time been depressed until he saw Bimar's father—only bored. But Bimar's father's black moods always seemed to affect Dilar.

Something brushed against his leg in the water, some-thing big, and he swam faster. Were there really such things as willimars? Grandfather was always claiming that he had seen one, seen a great fin above the water, or a huge tentacle stealing alongside the raft, or a big beak-like mouth opening to tear the nets and let the fishes escape right into its jaws.

Dilar had never seen any such thing. Never. Not even a shadow.

But it would be rather exciting if such a thing did exist, he admitted to himself. It would make swimming from raft to raft an adventure.

Now he walked the long raft from end to end, rather than running. At the far end he slipped quietly into the water and swam to his own craft. As he grasped the edge he noticed again that the outermost log was rotting, and a little piece of it came away in his fingers. Several times lately he had seen his father looking at that log in a worried fashion.

He ran his hands over his fishskin pants and swept the

water from them. Grandfather didn't like to have him come near the cooking fire when he was wet. It was hard enough to keep a fire going without Dilar dripping into it, he complained.

When he was as dry as he could make himself, Dilar sat down beside his grandfather, who handed him a bowl of fish stew.

"Where is Bimar?" he asked.

"Working," answered Dilar. He swallowed some stew. Perhaps he should have stayed here and helped his own father instead of going to entice Bimar to race with him. But they had fish in plenty, dried and fresh, and skin bags full of oil, and a pile of torches. If his father was now busy hauling in a net full of fish, it was surely because he had nothing else to do.

He ate the rest of his stew in silence and then went to the edge of the raft and rinsed out his bowl, made of a big shell. He squatted there, watching the rough stone walls slide past and slide past and slide past. The same and the same. . . . His eyes narrowed. That rock, that odd-shaped one with the reddish markings sticking out there. . . .

He carried his bowl back to the fire. His grandfather took it from him and stowed it in its proper place. Grandfather had a proper place for everything. Sometimes Dilar teased the old man, saying that his grandfather hated mealtime since it meant taking the bowls out of their proper place. But now Dilar only watched somberly and said nothing.

"Did you see a willimar?" asked Grandfather after a while. He was only making conversation, Dilar knew.

For a few seconds he went on looking at the old man and then he spoke.

"Grandfather," he asked softly, "where are we going?"

The old man busied himself feeding the fire with shreds of dried fish. "To a Better Place," he answered at last.

"A better place than what?" insisted Dilar.

The old man looked agitated. "A better place than where we were before," he said uneasily.

Dilar scowled. How would they know? Who remembered where they were before? Grandfather's grandfather had claimed to remember it. But he had died long before Dilar was born. All that Grandfather could remember of what his grandfather had told him was something about "green." And something else about "day."

"I do not believe," said Dilar slowly, "that we are going anywhere, Grandfather. I think we go around and around and around. I think we pass the same caves and the same cliffs time after time."

"Hush, hush!" cried the old man. "What wicked things to say. It is not true. You'll see. I myself mean to live to see that Better Place."

"Dilar!"

Dilar jumped. He knew his father didn't like to have him upset Grandfather. And yet he had not truly planned to excite the old man. It had seemed to him an important thing to think about and to ask about. He had talked of it once or twice to Bimar, but the whole thing had seemed to bewilder the other boy and Dilar had given up.

And who was there to ask otherwise? Not his father, who never answered questions, but just went on drawing up net after net of fish.

He had a net full now. "Come and help," he called, and Dilar sprang up and went to haul the net aboard the raft. There were three big fish and a dozen or so smaller ones caught in it. Dilar's father bent quickly and with his stone knife severed their spines, one by one.

"We'll take these to Mimal and Limar," he said, straightening up.

Mimal and Limar shared the raft, one of the smallest, with Dilar and his father and grandfather. They were an old couple whose only child had married and gone to live on the second raft in the procession. Limar was frail and he often was not able to fish; Gimal, Dilar's father, made a habit of taking a net full of fish to them every so often.

Now as Dilar followed him past the piles of fishskins and torches, Gimal said gently, "Don't torment your grandfather. He's old and such teasing isn't good for him."

"I wasn't teasing," said Dilar abruptly. "I wanted to know. Do *you* think we are headed for some Better Place?"

Gimal did not answer. He walked on carrying the net.

After Gimal had eaten and his bowl had been put into its proper place, the shell trumpet blew for sleep. The cooking fire was put out, and all the torches except one in the middle of the raft. Dilar lay down on the pallet of dried waterweeds which he had made for himself. He had never liked sleeping on fishskins.

But he was not sleepy. He lay watching the faint light flicker around him and hearing the water whisper and gurgle softly under his head.

He was a fool. There were a dozen ways he could have

found out for certain. Once he and Bimar had swum way ahead of the rafts, far out of the reach of all the torches, and had climbed up on a shelf of rocks and sat there in the dimness until the rafts had come floating up. If he had made a mark on that shelf, or piled stones, or anything, he could have seen it if they ever passed that way again. Even if no one else believed him, he would have known. He would have known for certain.

But he was fairly certain anyway. It was the others he wanted to convince. A thousand marks on the walls, a thousand piles of stones would not make Grandfather admit they were headed for nothing and nowhere. It would take something much more than stones.

The roof of the passage sloped down until, for a hundred feet or so, it was so low Dilar might almost have touched it with his hand had he been standing up. How often he had seen it do that! Were there really so many low places in this long, long winding cave that led them on and on?

Wasn't it the same low place that they passed over and over again, never realizing that it was the same one?

He turned restlessly and the dry weeds rustled under him. For a long while he lay there hearing the water and thinking.

They were coming now to a narrow place in the tunnel; the water ran more swiftly and noisily. The wall on one side came so close to the raft that Dilar felt sure he could simply step onto that narrow ledge, just barely visible.

And then suddenly he sprang up. He seized a fishnet and a torch. Swiftly he lit the torch at the one remaining alive on the raft, ran to the edge, and jumped up onto the rim of rock. For a moment he had to struggle for balance, but then there he was safe on the ledge. The raft slid away from him and there was darkness for a space, and then the following raft appeared. Dilar watched it going by, with the lumpy shapes of the sleeping people. It too disappeared, and then another raft slipped by and another. Dilar stared at it, clutching the torch. It glided on, silent and still, and Dilar's heart thumped painfully in his chest.

The raft was going by, was going by, was gone. The darkness deepened, and then nothing came to lighten it. Only shadows and the rushing of water. The last of the flotilla had drifted by and nothing, nothing, nothing could call it back.

CHAPTER 2

Dilar crouched on the ledge of rock staring down the tunnel at the point where the frail gleam of the last torch had disappeared. He had done it, for once and all. For a long time he stared into the twilight imagining how it would be when the Raft People came that way again and found him on his rock wall. What would Grandfather say? And Bimar? Would it make Grandfather laugh for once? Or would he be sadder than ever?

The torch fluttered and the little flame, which had not yet caught properly, almost died. Dilar sprang up from his dreaming and looked at it anxiously. And suddenly he was frightened half out of his wits. Suppose he was wrong? Suppose the rafts never came this way again? Suppose he must live for the rest of his life on this narrow shelf, never to see another human being again?

He drew a deep breath and held it, to keep the panic from rising up in his throat and making him scream. There was no use in screaming. Those on the rafts might hear, but what good would that do?

He could try to swim after them. The current here was so strong it would carry him faster than he could swim. But it carried the rafts quickly too. He had waited too long. He would never catch up with them. He would grow exhausted and drown in the rough water without even coming within sight of the procession.

No. He had behaved stupidly, like fish that in panic sometimes swim into the nets instead of away from them. But he was alive. He had fire and a net. The river teemed with fish. His people had long ago learned to make use of every fish scale and strand of weed in the river. He could keep himself alive until. . . .

Until the rafts came around again, he told himself firmly. He knew it was true: they would come again. It was not only that he had noticed the same caves and rocks, but also that he read the answer in Gimal's eyes, in Bimar's father's black looks, in a dozen ways. . . .

He examined his torch, a great snail shell wedged into a split in a big fishbone. The shell was filled with bits of dried fish organs and water plants soaked with fish oil. The torches did not make a very bright light, but they burned a long time. Now Dilar stirred the oil and blew gently on the weeds to make his burn more steadily. Then he walked along the narrow platform of rock, exploring as best he could by the dim light.

At first he walked in the direction of the current, but after a few minutes he turned resolutely around. The rafts would come from the other direction when they returned. He would walk to meet them as far as the stone path would allow him.

It allowed him a good distance, far more than the length of one of the long rafts. The way was uneven and full of cracks; he stumbled often and pebbles hurt his feet. But he went on until the ledge grew so narrow that he worried about falling into the water and putting out his torch. He was tired. First he would sleep and then

when he woke he would set about making better arrange-
ments for himself. He would catch fish, to eat and to
dry, and more important, to use for fuel. He would build
a fire on the ledge and then take the torch and search as
far as he could in either direction. Then if he fell in the
river with his torch it would be no matter, he would still
have fire.

He retraced his steps until he found what seemed to be
the widest part of his ledge. He wedged the torch into
a crack and inspected it to see that it would keep burning
even if he slept a long while. He believed it would.

At last he lay down to sleep. But how hard and cold
the rock beneath him was! And how strange the water
sounded lapping and lipping against the wall, not running and murmuring under the raft logs.

Wasn't it better to go around and around in the company of his people than to stay still forever alone? Alone,
alone, alone. . . . He sat up in sudden despair and anger,
and heard scurrying noises and felt something brush over
his hand. He leaped to his feet and glared about him.

In the dimness he could see them crowding along the
stone shelf, sliding over each other, leaping up the cave
wall. Sharp-nosed, hump-shouldered, naked-tailed . . .
when they came close enough to the light their eyes
gleamed evilly, red with rage.

Dilar had glimpsed them once or twice before, watching from the walls. He had not known what they were,
nor did any of the other Raft People. Once in a great
while one of the creatures would drop into the water and
swim alongside the flotilla, and Grandfather said they
even came aboard the rafts, when everyone was asleep.

Grandfather was afraid of them, and Bimar's mother,

for their ugly, hateful looks and sharp teeth and scaly tails.

And now all at once Dilar too was a little frightened of them. There were hundreds, thousands of them, just outside the ring of faint light from his torch, pouring restlessly back and forth, the strange slithering sound of their bodies filling his ears and making him shiver. Once in a while there would be a shrill squeal or a sharp clitter. Dilar looked around for a rock to throw. There were only pebbles.

He leaned over and snatched up his torch. The creatures fell back a little but in the brighter light Dilar achieved by holding his torch higher he saw more and more of them hurrying toward him. They crowded on the ledge, pushing and shoving, and once in a while there was a splash as one fell in.

What did they want of him? Dilar asked himself. They were different from fish, he could tell that. Thousands of fish might crowd around him in the water, nibbling at his legs, tickling along his spine, and he might grow annoyed at them, might kick out and splash to drive them away.

But he was not afraid of them. The sight of them did not give him a sudden spasm of loathing somewhere in his stomach the way the sight of these things and their long yellow teeth did.

Whatever they wanted of him, it wasn't anything good.

Now either they were pushing forward more strongly or they were growing bolder. Inch by inch the nearer ones were creeping toward him. Their eyes blazed fiercely. Dilar waved the torch and tried to shout at them, but he was too terrified. His voice strings made no answer to his orders and he merely gaped.

The things came closer; Dilar backed toward the wall. One of them darted in at him and this time he did yell and leaped back a foot, only to brush against one hanging on the wall. He turned and almost flung the torch at the creature; he had all he could do to keep it clutched in his hand. Whatever happened he must not lose his fire.

They were crowding him back to the wall. He couldn't stand to have them touch him. He pressed against the rock glancing up to see if any of them were clinging to it above his head.

There was a crevice in the wall to one side of him, a deep crack. If he slid into the crack, it would keep the things from approaching him from right and left, anyway. He crammed himself into the opening and only then, wedged in, did it occur to him that there might be others in there with him. Hastily he turned sideways and tried to touch the back of the narrow slot, but his exploring hand found only empty air. The creatures, seeing him retreat, surged forward and he squeezed himself further into the crevice and touched a smooth boulder and then suddenly he was all the way inside the narrow little cave and climbing up. He pressed against the stone and hitched himself up on his feet and elbows and his bottom. He still clutched the torch, and looking down, he could see the things trickling into the cave after him.

Could they climb up here? Perhaps. They seemed able to climb almost anything. The boulder felt smooth to him but no doubt they could find claw holds. He inched slowly to the top and behind him there was another of the tall, smooth, rounded rocks. He tried to see where he was and what was around him, but the shadows and flickering light confused him. The only way open seemed to be up. There was a scratchy sound and the narrow, wicked heads and gleaming eyes of the things showed over the rim of the stone.

The boulder at Dilar's back was steeper and harder to climb. He dared not turn his back on the creatures, but slid backward up this stone too, still holding the torch. He struggled on and once slipped and thought he was going to land right in the middle of all those claws and teeth, but managed to stop himself.

Away from the water the sounds of the beasts were louder than ever, their cries and angry chatter, and the sound of fur brushing across fur, which set Dilar's teeth on edge, and the scrabble of their claws on rock. They were flooding into the crevice now and scrambling all around him and he yelled out in horror; for a minute they were all frozen as his voice resounded monstrously in that narrow space. But when the echoes died they came on, thousands of them, closer and closer, and he climbed steadily, though he trembled all over.

Something clawed at his foot, something scrabbled at his ankle. In terror and desperation he flung the torch down among them. The squeaks and chippers rose to a shriek and, both his hands free now, he climbed fast, fast, panting and half sobbing. After a minute or so the air around him felt different, the rocks felt wet and slippery. He did not know what he was coming to, but he climbed through the darkness hoping for any sort of help. And suddenly he felt space about him; the air was damp and cool and fresh, different from any he had ever breathed before. It was dark, darker far than the tunnel. He could stand up at last. He stretched out his arms and felt nothing. The rocks still rose slightly beneath his feet, but gradually they gave way to something soft and sandy and then to something strange and yielding, strands of something that whispered and bent beneath his feet.

The things had left him. The air was full of noises, curious sounds he had never heard before and couldn't imagine the source of. But there was about them nothing ominous or evil as there had been about the sounds of the things.

He walked a long way, holding his hands in front of him, stumbling occasionally over rocks and other objects, but finding nothing he could take hold of and nothing he could identify. There were no rock walls anywhere, no river, no cliffs; nothing solid except the stuff on which he cautiously put his feet. The wetness was all around him, but he was accustomed to wetness. And at last, exhausted, he lay down and fell asleep, not daring to think what he would do when he woke, or how he would get along without fire or how he would ever get back to the rafts and the river.

When he awoke, he could only suppose he had died.

The darkness was beginning to lift. Opening his eyes he looked straight up into the pale mists and clouds drifting away: pearly, shining softly, billowing and rolling, letting him glimpse every now and then the endless, depthless, timeless, vast blue curve of the sky. . . .

CHAPTER 3

He lay there without moving. Once he had had a dream in which he had beheld the blaze of many thousand torches, so that the flickering shadows and darkness had disappeared. But in that dream he had seen only the narrow walls and low ceilings of the tunnel. No dream had ever told him there was this infinite, enormous light-filled nothingness, near enough to touch yet so far away a lifetime's travel would bring you no closer to its end.

The light grew brighter and Dilar turned his head to find its source: a huge red ball hanging in the clouds just over the edge of the world. It hurt his eyes to look at it and he turned his head in the other direction.

He was lying in the middle of a great expanse of something which he could not have named, rather like the waterweeds that floated in the river. Only these things were fastened to the sand and mud underneath them and they were of a color Dilar had only glimpsed on the sides of certain fishes shining in the glow of the torches, or when the eyes of the long-legged spiders reflected the flames as the big spinners hung from the rocks, as they did once in a great while.

The color was green. Dilar knew it suddenly. This was what Grandfather's grandfather had meant, this lively color, soft yet brilliant, spreading out underfoot and crawling up onto all the strange-looking things scattered around here and there. And there, far over there, those tall things, gray and smooth and round. Their top parts were laden with this green, their heads swathed in it, their outstretched arms carrying huge burdens of it.

Were these things alive? They moved gently. Dilar scrambled to his feet and made his way slowly toward them. He heard no sound; only the air stirred softly as he had known it to do when the tunnel branched or a big cave gaped in the wall. Watching the tall objects ahead of him he decided it was the wind that made them move. They were not alive after all.

When he came close he was not so sure. Something about them was alive. Putting his hand on those warm, gray bodies he was certain that they were living. But they would not be things to fear. He knew that.

The green stuff grew out of them, in little flat flakes with tiny handles. The flakes were smooth and cool to touch. Were they like fish scales, only larger and softer? Dilar wondered. No, the rough surface of those bodies must be like fish scales, he told himself, and tried to prove it by breaking off a piece. The stuff underneath was familiar to him and suddenly he knew what these creatures were.

They were logs! Round and straight and made of wood. Somehow, sometime, somewhere, Grandfather's grandfather's father and all the rest must have knocked these things down and stripped them of their outer cover and fastened them together to make the rafts.

And surely then this was the very spot they had left

for a "Better Place"! But how could anyone want a better place than this? As he walked under the trees, Dilar marveled. Light and space were enough to make this the most beautiful and amazing place that anyone could dream of.

Beyond the grove of trees the land sloped steeply downward. Dilar was a little scared. It seemed a strange thing for the world to do, tipping on its side so that everything must slide to a heap at the bottom.

Nothing seemed to be sliding. A line of low trees crept down the hill and Dilar made up his mind that he would go beside them, to catch hold of them if he started falling.

He cried out abruptly. Something was coming toward him in the air, a little fish gliding through the air, helping itself along with great fins that stuck out from its sides and them folded tight against them. A wonder, a wonder! The fish stopped suddenly in the top of one of the little trees, put out little legs to hold itself up, threw back its head, and opening its mouth made such sounds as Dilar had never heard before. No water murmured so joyously or so sweetly or so triumphantly; nothing, nothing had ever rung upon his ears like that or made his heart feel it must burst open with that song's wild delight. Even when it had ceased it echoed in his head.

The fish flew up and out of sight and Dilar put his hand to his head. He was dizzy with marvels. Who would have guessed; who would have dreamed?

The sun shone upon him as he faltered down the hillside, the clouds were almost gone. The warmth fell pleasantly upon his skin, the grass smelled delicious.

Several big white things that he had supposed were big stones lying about the field had got up on small legs and begun to move around. Dilar stopped. Two of them came close and looked at him with gentle, rather stupid faces and then began again to nuzzle at the green grass. He wondered if all this lovely world belonged to these fluffy creatures, if they were the only inhabitants except the green-bearing logs.

Was Dilar the only man in all this beautiful land?

"Hey," he said to one of the white things, and it answered "Baaa!" and trotted quickly away. Dilar stared after it feeling a little forlorn.

The light was growing brighter and brighter. It hurt his eyes fiercely and he kept within the shade of the little trees as much as he was able. Something under the trees smelled wonderful; it made his mouth water though it was like nothing he had ever tasted. The smell seemed to come not from the greenery or from the bodies of the trees but from the small roundish pink and yellow objects which hung from them and sometimes fell softly to the ground.

Dilar picked one up and examined it. The skin seemed to his fingers to have tiny hairs all over it, but the object itself was soft and rather squashy. He squeezed gently and the skin split and juice spurted out over his hand. At first he was horrified, for he supposed this thing was living, but after a bit he concluded that since it had fallen from the branch it was probably dead.

He started to wipe the juice from his hand but it smelled so delicious he stopped. He was hungry. He had had nothing to eat since his fish-stew supper, and much had happened since then. He looked carefully at the fruit. Would it harm him to eat it? He touched his tongue tentatively to the juice.

He laughed aloud in delight. He had not imagined there was such a taste! Suddenly he felt that he had spent all his life aching for the flavor of whatever this was. He bit into the peach and ate it all in seconds, not even being slowed down by the big rough seed on which his teeth had closed jarringly at the second bite. Better to die eating something so deliciously poisonous than to die of starvation, he told himself. For he had no idea what in this strange country might be wholesome and what might not.

He picked up a dozen of these objects from the grass and ate them all. Afterward his stomach felt a little odd. Perhaps these things had indeed poisoned him? He waited to die, but though he suffered some sharp pains he did not seem to be dying. He sat down in the deepest shade he could find, for he found the bright light too warm on his skin and agonizing to his eyes, and wondered whether his father and grandfather would ever know what had happened to him. One of the singing fishes lit above him and murmured sweetly, a pleasant, soft warble, almost like the sound of water running, and by and by Dilar fell asleep.

When he woke he concluded that he had in truth been poisoned and was dying. He was on fire all over, his eyes were so swollen he could barely squint through the lids, in his mouth his tongue was thick and swollen with thirst and venom. He touched his face, finding it, too, puffy and feverish, and wherever his fingers brushed his flesh, flames seemed to follow them and sear the skin.

He staggered to his feet, and began to stumble around, half out of his mind with fear and pain. Oh, why had he thought to leave the raft, where he was safe and comfortable? Oh, who would help him in this alien place, this country of fantasy? Not the white woolly things he had seen earlier, he was certain. They were too stupid to help. But when he glimpsed three or four of them, through his watering eyes, he could not stop himself; he went toward them, half falling, reeling, making eerie, gargling noises between his cracked lips.

The sheep grazed peacefully, only moving a little farther from him and a little farther and a little farther, each time he came near. He stood still at last, hopeless, exhausted, frightened, and angry. He heard voices then, voices such as the Raft People had, not the foolish flat voices of the white four-legged beasts. He could even make out a word or two, it seemed to him.

He turned in that direction, waving his arms, and uttering hoarse, gasping cries that sounded strange even to his own ears. He could see men, he was sure those blurred figures were men, and he wailed piteously.

The voices ceased. Then suddenly they began again, shouts louder than his own, shouts of fear and anger. Something struck him sharply on the shoulder, and then something else crashed into his forehead, and he realized that the men were throwing stones at him.

He stood still, weeping, holding his arms over his head to protect himself, begging for help, while the shower of rocks stopped and there was a sound of running and then silence, and he knew he was alone again.

"Come back! Come back!" he pleaded. "Help me, help me!"

But no one answered and at last he sank to the ground, stunned and faint, and sat there for a long time, moaning and sobbing, without knowing he was doing it, thinking once when he heard the sounds that there must be someone else close by, tortured and suffering as he was.

Someone touched him gently on his shoulder and the fire of that touch jerked him back to awareness. He looked up and could make out a face looking down into his.

"My name is Dorna," said a girl's voice. "Do not move. I will fetch my mother and she will help you."

CHAPTER 4

"Come away, Grandfather!" he pleaded. "Come away. It is so bright, so bright. It is a Better Place, Grandfather; there is green there, everything is green. A ball of light overhead, like a million torches. Come away!"

"Why, boy, we have a million torches. See, I've lit this one and this one, see how many. I'll light another and another!"

"Grandfather, it's too many; it's too hot!"

"Now, this is a Better Place," the old man shouted. "Now, this is the brightest place in all the world. And we'll light more torches and more torches. . . ."

"Grandfather, I'm too hot, I'm on fire, I'm burning, burning, burning. . . ." Dilar gasped, and cool hands seized him gently and a voice said, "Drink, drink!" A bowl was pressed to his lips and he drank, something cool and pleasant, and he lay down and slipped into blackness as though he had been swallowed by a willi-mar. . . .

The fishes swam around him, one of them sang in a low, sweet voice. But now they were changing, changing into big furry things with red eyes and bare tails and pointed noses. Their teeth were long and yellow and one of them spoke suddenly, saying, "Here he is, we have found him at last—eat his skin, eat his skin, eat his skin."

And another said, "A Better Place, a Better Place, a Better Place," and they came at him, their great teeth scraped over his skin, over his arms and shoulders, and he screamed, but then he heard the woman's voice again, saying, "Be still, be still," and though her touch was agony, the salve she was applying took away the pain shortly and he slept again.

He could not open his eyes. He lay without moving and heard the woman's voice and a man's voice, but could not see them or anything else.

"He seems to be mending," the man said and the woman replied, "Oh, yes. He's young and strong. The fever's nearly gone now, and the blisters are healing. His shoulders and face were the worst, but I am a fair doctor. I think he will soon be good as new."

"I could wonder where he came from," said the man in an awed tone.

There was a long pause. And finally the woman said, "I think he is one of the Raft People."

The man shouted with laughter. "Oh, no, Norna, what an idea. The Raft People are only myth, something made up by grandmothers and grandfathers to tell children on a winter's evening."

"He must be," said the woman. "Tell me where else he could come from. Look, this is what he was wearing, fishskin. He reeked of fish. And who else would have such skin, so pale that a few hours in the spring sunshine would burn it so. Where it was not burned, it is whiter than milk, whiter than snow. If he had not been by nature dark complexioned, he would have died."

Borba growled. "I couldn't believe such a tale. I

couldn't. He would have to lead me by the hand and show me the rafts and the river. And even then I'd doubt that such things could be. . . ."

"Perhaps he will tell us when he wakes, Borba, if he wants," said the woman's voice, and then there was silence.

Dilar lay listening. The talk made his head swim. What did those words mean—snow, milk, spring? He could understand the rest of their speech, though some of the words sounded slurred and strange. Perhaps he was dreaming the whole thing; perhaps he was still lying on the raft with Gimal and the others, never having left. Surely there was no such place as this and no such people. What had happened to him and why was he here, if this were not a dream? Ah, he was afraid and worried, and by and by fear and worry made him so tired that once again he drifted off to sleep. . . .

"What is this I'm eating?" he asked Dorna.

"Eggs," she answered.

"Eggs?" he cried. "What kind of fish lays eggs like this?"

"Not a fish, silly, a hen," she told him.

"A hen? What is a hen?"

"A hen is—a hen," she said impatiently. "You don't know *anything!*"

"I don't know what I know," he answered unhappily, but Dorna did not hear. She had turned away and was looking off across the grass. "There!" she said, "there by the pear tree. Those things are hens."

Dilar lifted his eyes from the fascinating dish of boiled

eggs and squinted at the hens. Though he was sitting in deep shade, looking into the light made his eyes water. He stared anyway. He could not resist staring at all these new and wonderful things: eggs, hens, pots made of iron, cloth woven of sheep's wool, pear trees, butterflies, grass, and weeds—all these things made him gasp in astonishment. And if he lived to be as old as Grandfather's grandfather, he would never get over the breathless miracle of the sun and sky. He had not dared yet to look at the sun again. But in the twilight he stood every night to watch its splendor fade from the horizon; to see the stars surface out of the dusk like little gleaming fish; to wait for the moon to rise and hang in space, pale and cool, opening night by night from a silver stalk to a wide, white blossom. Now it was beginning to slowly close again.

"Now, see," said Dorna penitently. "Looking has made your eyes water. And they are only ugly old hens."

"They are beautiful," said Dilar. "It is all beautiful."

He wanted to know more about the hens, but he did not ask. These people hardly ever asked questions, and never personal ones. Strangers were always greeted as Dorna had greeted him—"My name is Dorna"—so that newcomers might be spared the pain of asking even so much as a name. No one had asked him who he was or where he came from and in his turn he tried not to question Norna and Dorna too much. If he did, Dorna quickly grew impatient and Norna gave him strange looks, as though he should know better.

Besides, in time he found answers himself and he felt that was best. He knew that most of his questions must seem foolish as well as rude to Norna and Dorna.

He had learned that he was right about "green," about

the logs called trees being alive, he had learned about "day" and about "night," and that there were times called summer, winter, spring, and fall. He could not imagine what they were nor why Dorna looked discontent when she spoke about winter.

"Come," she said now. "We'll go up by the meadows and pick grapes. I know a way that is in the shade, there and back, except for a little, little bit."

"He must wear a hat," said Norna quickly, from the doorway. "And I will fix an eyeshade for him. And he must keep his arms covered."

Dilar hated keeping his arms covered. His sunburn was almost healed, but every day Norna smeared him with lotions and salves, some to heal, some to toughen his skin. Then when he put on the long-sleeved shirt she insisted on, the cloth stuck to the greasy salves and clung to his shoulders and back and felt horrible to a boy who had never before in his whole life worn anything but a pair of short fishskin breeches. But he was so anxious to leave his seat under the trees and get out into this beautiful and unbelievable world that he would have endured much worse.

Every day he spent so many minutes in the sun. Soon his skin would be whole again, Norna said, and strengthened to stand the touch of the sun without a shirt and all the lotions.

But he must wear for a while longer the brimmed hat and the eyeshade woven of dried grass. Norna was worried that he might injure his eyes again. "Skin will replace itself, but eyes won't," she warned. "You'd best take care."

Now swaddled and sweating in his shirt and his salves,

Dilar followed Dorna under the fragrant fruit trees, along a worn path. Every now and then Dorna stopped to pick a pear or a plum or an apricot and offer it to him. He ate them all. Sometimes it seemed to him that he never did anything but eat. Who could have imagined there were such things to eat? Tomatoes and berries, beans and squash, melons and potatoes—and honey, which he could only eat a drop at a time for its sweetness made tears come to his eyes and his throat close up. Every mouthful he ate astonished and delighted him, who had never before eaten anything but fish and snails and waterweeds.

Dorna could not help laughing at him. That these simple fruits and vegetables, so commonplace they were not even planted or cultivated but seeded and cared for themselves in the hedgerows and meadows and wayside ditches, should so fill him with awe amazed her. She searched every day for something new to give him, to watch his surprise and pleasure at the sight and feel and taste of it. To see him eating his first strawberry was, she said, enough to make a pumpkin laugh.

And Dilar said only, "What is a pumpkin?"

"Now here is the only place without shade," she told him suddenly. "Shut your eyes and give me your hand. We'll run, over there, to the shade of those big trees at the top of the slope."

Dilar squinted up the hill. He recognized this place. With a sudden heart-leaping anguish he knew that this was the grove of trees he had entered that very first morning in this world. He must have come toward it from the other direction and down from the mountain there where it was rocky and bare. Someplace up among the stony outcroppings must be the way back to the caves and the tunnel and the rafts.

"Now run!" ordered Dorna, and he ran, squeezing his eyes almost shut and letting her guide him. When they reached the grove, he was panting and sweating. He got hot much more quickly than Dorna or any of these people.

"It is better than cold," Dorna always said, and he could not answer her, for he didn't know what cold was. Heat he knew, from the fish-oil fires and the torches. He had burned himself often enough on a hot bowl of fish stew. But cold, what was cold? Dorna held his hand in the spring that purled up out of the rocks on the mountainside. "That's cold," she said. So he knew what cold was. But he could not imagine cold all around him, like a cloak, pressing against his face and arms and back, the way the heat did.

Today even Dorna complained of the heat and wiped the drops of sweat from her face with a hand stained with plum juice and dust. Suddenly she smiled and waved. "There are Borba and Forlan and Katran," she said, but the three shepherds did not wave back. Instead they pretended to be staring off up the mountain, and then turned away. Dorna laughed gleefully. "They are playing that they don't see us," she cried. "They are still ashamed because they were frightened of you and threw stones and ran. I wasn't afraid," she boasted.

Dilar said nothing. He could not blame the shepherds. He had been a terrible sight: naked, blind, crimson, swollen-faced. Had he met such a creature stumbling and wailing in the twilight he too might have thrown stones.

But the tale always reminded him that he owed his life to Dorna and her mother. He wanted to think of some way to repay them, though in truth they had not seemed to suppose that he owed them anything.

At the moment anyway he had no time to think of it. He kept blinking around, trying to decide where he had come out of the mountainside.

The mountain was not as high as the mountains on the other side of the valley, the Mountains of the Tigers, as Norna and Dorna called them. Sheep grazed almost to the top. There was a pass where they sometimes strayed through and onto the far slope, a gentle pasture falling slowly to the sea, miles away, but very poor and rocky. No one lived there and even the sheep soon came back home, not liking the few mouthfuls of tough, salty grass they found there.

But Dilar had come out on this side of the mountain. And though he searched with his eyes all up the slope he could not see any crack or cave or crevice which might offer an entrance into the depths of the earth.

Dorna led the way through the woods till they came to a place where the trees were looped and hung with vines. Bunches of fruit, deep red and blue-green, dangled from the vines. Not yet ripe, she told Dilar. "What do you mean?" he asked, and Dorna struggled to explain. "Not yet old enough to eat," she said, and picked one of the grapes and popped it into his mouth. The tart juice, a fresh, sharp taste, made his mouth draw up a little and he chewed thoughtfully. "Delicious," he said, and Dorna was disgusted.

A week later Dilar rose one morning in the first light,

when the birds were only stirring and Dorna and her mother both slept peacefully on their cots. Softly he made his way out of the house, without the shirt and the salves and the hat and the sunshade, and took the faint path up the mountainside. He went beyond the thin woods and up the shaly slope he had come down that very first misty morning. He was sure this was the way he had come.

Somewhere under his feet curled the river which had been all his life. Right now, this very minute, below this spot where he stood, the flotilla might be making its slow, dark, futile way, around and around, silent between the walls of rock.

"Grandfather," he cried aloud. "Grandfather! It is day here; it is green. I will come and bring you out into this better place."

A bird sang in answer, a clear and fragile sound like water dropping into a pool. But though Dilar searched for three hours, back and forth along the hillside, till the sun was high in the sky and strong enough to dazzle and burn his eyes, he found no crack nor cave nor crevice that might let anyone in or out of the heart and veins of that mountain.

CHAPTER 5

"We will take Borba's donkey," said Dorna. "She is stubborn, but she doesn't bite and kick."

Dilar wondered how Dorna would know which was Borba's donkey, for like the sheep and hens they wandered where they willed, without any identifying marks that he could see, and whoever needed a donkey simply took the one at hand.

Dorna knew where the donkeys would be, and when she and Dilar found them, she had no trouble picking out Borba's little gray one. She grabbed it by one ear and tugged it along. It came amiably enough, only stopping every now and then to grab a mouthful of grass or leaves as it went.

They followed a path to Forlan's house. A narrow wooden sledge leaned against the shed behind his house and they fastened the donkey to it while Forlan's little boy, round eyed and silent, watched them.

It was strange, Dilar thought. On the rafts no one ever touched anyone else's property. Here everybody's donkey was anybody's donkey. When Norna needed wool she ran out and sheared the first sheep she came to, though once a woman Dilar did not know had come to Norna with a dozen eggs, saying she had sheared one of Norna's sheep and found its wool of such fine quality that she wanted to give Norna the eggs.

Norna was a doctor. Behind her house she grew a garden of herbs and simples and she knew how to use them and how to preserve them. She often went to tend those who were sick or hurt, but she did not seem to think she was owed anything for her services. It was what she could do and she did it.

"Come along, do," said Dorna impatiently to the donkey, which had found a succulent patch of yellow flowers and wanted to eat them all before continuing the journey. It was Dorna's intention to go a long way down the valley where pumpkins grew large and smooth and golden. Dilar suspected they would go only as far as the donkey wished to take them, and he was right. Once the little beast had finished the yellow flowers and finally agreed to set out along the path, it went exactly where it wished to go, stepping briskly along for a couple of miles and then stopping. No amount of urging and slapping and pushing and tugging could move it. Dorna shrugged her shoulders. "Ah, well," she said, "these pumpkins look very fine." And they began to load them on the sledge.

To Dilar one pumpkin looked very like another. The valley was full of them; they lay in ditches and cluttered hillsides and huddled in the meadow grass like so many stones. There were so many it seemed to Dilar that the country was drowning in pumpkins.

"What a lot of pumpkins!" he exclaimed.

Dorna shrugged again. "It is the way of pumpkins," she answered. Her face darkened. "It is not always so.

Some years there is a blight. We had a donkey once, my mother and I, but it died during the winter after the last blight."

"Did it die of the blight?" asked Dilar, and she stamped her foot impatiently at him. "Don't be silly. A donkey couldn't have a pumpkin blight. He died of not having enough to eat. In the winter when there's snow on the ground, pumpkins are all the animals have to eat."

So that's why we are gathering these pumpkins! thought Dilar triumphantly. Once again he had found the answer to a question without asking. He wished he dared ask more questions, especially about winter. What was this winter, this sad and terrible time? How could he stay with Norna and Dorna and eat their food when they might not have enough for themselves? And where could he go? He could not find his way back to his own people; he had searched and searched for the way back. But he must not stay here, he was sure of that.

He picked up another pumpkin and put it on the sledge. The donkey was eating grass and Dorna was gathering mushrooms. Dilar worked away by himself and soon had the sledge piled high. "How do you get this donkey to move?" he called to Dorna. She glanced around and laughed. "With a load that heavy you may even have to pull the sledge yourself," she answered. "Give the donkey a kick or two."

But Dilar talked to the donkey and tickled its ears and shoved and pushed and finally it started homeward. Dorna walked by its head and every now and then fed it a handful of berries or a mushroom or a yellow flower to encourage it and keep it going.

Passing the lower meadows they heard shouts and Dorna ran to see who was there. A dozen young people were running about on the slopes, chasing the sheep away from the flat hollow in the center of the field. "Dancing!" cried Dorna. "Look, Gofran has his horn and someone's brought a harp. There's going to be dancing! Come along, Dilar!"

"What about the pumpkins?" he asked.

"Oh, leave them here," she said and shrugged her shoulders.

It was the way of these people, Dilar knew. If someone came along while they were gone and wanted the donkey, he'd take it; Dilar and Dorna would soon find another. If he wanted the pumpkins he'd take the pumpkins, for whoever had gathered these could easily gather more. It seemed a strange way of doing things, yet try as he might Dilar could not see anything truly wrong with it. For all those things were true: donkeys grazed here, there, and yon; anybody could find a sledge and use it; pumpkins could be gathered by the thousands.

"I will go on," he said. "I'll put the pumpkins in the shed. You go with the others."

"Why?" she wanted to know. "We don't have dancing every day."

Dilar smiled. "I think I'm very bad at dancing," he replied. "Anyway, I've started gathering the pumpkins. I always like to finish what I start."

"But if you stop doing something you *have* finished," cried Dorna, irked. Smiling suddenly she turned away from him. "Oh, well, do as you wish. I wouldn't miss dancing for anything."

Dilar followed the donkey and sledge along the edge of the meadow. In truth he would like to try dancing. All the people were good dancers. And the girls were all pretty. It made his heart lighter to watch them and hear their voices, full of laughter and music.

But he did not want to join the others. He could not feel happy and at ease with them. Though they were friendly and kind he could almost feel their eyes touching the scars on his cheeks and shoulders. Though they never asked questions he could see the questions always in their eyes.

He piled the pumpkins neatly in the rough shed at one side of Norna's house. She came running out to help him and showed him how to spread a little hay between and over the rows to keep the pumpkins dry and wholesome.

"Shall I fetch more?" he asked and she nodded. "Yes, we fill the shed full and it keeps the sheep very well. Last year there were enough to give Borba a few toward the end of the winter, for he has twelve sheep and finds it hard to feed them."

Dilar stared in surprise. "There are pumpkins in plenty," he said. "He should store enough for his sheep."

"Oh, he stores his shed quite full," said Norna. "It's just that twelve sheep eat a great deal."

"I could wonder why he doesn't build a bigger shed," Dilar stated carefully. This was, he now knew, the polite way to ask a question. "Or even two sheds." Now it was Norna's turn to look surprised. "He fills his shed full," she repeated, a little crossly, and Dilar knew it was useless.

The future was something these people did not seem able to think about. A shedful of pumpkins should feed the sheep and they simply could not comprehend that it would not be so. They seemed unable to imagine anything that had not already happened many times before. And even if they could imagine it, they did not actually believe what they imagined. Forethought was just not possible to them.

Dilar had learned this already. Listening to Dorna speak of the lack of food during the winter he had suggested that some of the fruits and vegetables might be dried for storage, for he remembered how his own people dried fish and fish and fish, against the day of shortage that never came.

Norna and Dorna had burst out laughing at this strange notion. Whoever heard of such a thing? Secretly Dilar had tried his plan himself. But the hens had eaten the first fruits he had spread in the sun. And so he had climbed to the flat roof of the house, where the hens seldom ventured, and laid out rows of apricots and pears and peaches, only to have them ruined by one of the sudden slashing storms that flayed the countryside in the middle of summer. So he had given up.

But it was a wonder to him, all the same, that no one of them seemed to try it. On the rafts the future was all people had thought of—the Better Place they were going to, the lack of food that might someday come, so that they stored up dried fish endlessly, what lay around the next turn in the tunnel—willimars or worse. He pondered these things while he filled the sledge again and followed the donkey back to the shed. Dorna and the others had disappeared from the lower meadows and he wondered where they had gone.

When the shed was full of glistening round pumpkins,

he took the sledge back to Forlan. While he was unfastening the donkey Forlan appeared among the trees at the back of his house. He and Borba and Katran were still a little uneasy with Dilar, remembering that first meeting and the stones they had flung. But Dilar always tried to be friendly, to show that he understood and harbored no grudge. Now he smiled. "I have brought back your sledge," he explained.

Forlan laughed. "It is not my sledge," he said and he bent to look at it. "And it is not Borba's sledge, nor Morlon's nor Katran's. Ah, see, one of the runners has been broken and mended. Now I know who has a sledge with a mended runner. Let me think. Oh, yes, Gorga; it is Gorga's sledge." He nodded in satisfaction. "Shall I take it to Gorga?" asked Dilar, and Forlan looked surprised. "I do not think Gorga is looking for it," he said finally. "If he wants it, no doubt he can find it here."

He offered Dilar a bowl of fruit juices mixed with honey and cooled in the stone well of his spring. It was a hot day and Dilar was grateful for the drink. Gorga's wife brought out some little cakes made of potatoes mixed with sheep's milk and fried in chicken fat. They were very good. Dilar and Forlan sat on two stones while they ate and drank. Dilar gazed up at the high mountains across the valley.

"I was wondering what lay beyond the mountain," he said.

Forlan shrugged. "I do not know," he replied. "I have never been there. It is hard to cross the mountains, for they are high and the ways are steep and rough. There are tigers everywhere. Some have been, but not I. Why

42

go to all that trouble just to go down on the other side. That's what I always say."

He took a deep drink from his bowl. "Though it is said that somewhere in those other lands there are wise men. The wisest in all the world. Some say they can answer any question." He shrugged again. "But the question never came up that has made me that eager to learn the answer."

Dilar scarcely heard. He was staring up into the mountains. He would go there then, up among the blue peaks. For he had questions and questions and questions, and it would take wise men indeed to answer them.

CHAPTER 6

The moon, which had been full, waned and then again began to grow and swell upon the surface of the sky. Things were changing, were different. The leaves hung dull and lackluster on the trees, the bees and wasps buzzed with a desperate drunken energy among the falling and rotting fruits, and no more apples or pears or grapes came to ripen on the branches and vines. The days grew shorter, the nights made Dilar shiver. Winter was coming.

Every morning Dilar woke with a small mouse of worry chewing away at his heart. Every morning he lay on his cot pondering what he should do. Was this the day when he would get up his courage and leave the house of Norna and Dorna, as he had stepped from the raft and left his father and grandfather?

He must go soon. Winter would be hard enough for Norna and Dorna without another mouth to feed. But where would he go? Should he search for those wise men who might tell him what to do? Perhaps he should search instead for the way back to the river and the rafts? If he found it, he might not go back. He had come out into the living world and he intended to stay. But, oh, he would like to see Grandfather again, to bring him too out into the sun and show him this Better Place.

But where would he go now? It was different from leaving the rafts, a thing done and over in a few minutes, only one thing to do. Every day he waited for something to happen that would help him know what to do.

And then one morning when he went to pour water from the pitcher that was kept by the door to wash with, the water would not flow. Instead it hung in the vessel and when he touched the surface it was cold and hard. He was astounded and even a little afraid. Water that would not pour? He poked at it again and it broke and he picked up one of the pieces and held it till it burned his fingers.

Was this what winter did then, made this rigid strange covering over everything? Made the world flame and scorch in this upside-down fashion, burn with cold instead of heat? The ice melted and drops ran down his hands and fell on the floor. When Dorna picked up the pitcher she cried out, "Ice!" in such an anguished voice that Dilar trembled to hear her.

He thought that day might be spent in some kind of lamentation for the lost summer, but no, life went as usual. Norna swept the rooms and aired the beds; Dorna and Dilar scrubbed the breakfast bowls and gathered fruits and nuts and dug potatoes for the day's meals. Then Dilar set off on a task of his own.

Dorna's father had died three winters before, out in the snow searching for firewood. He had gone too far and grown too weary and somewhere along the way home had fallen on a rough hillside and frozen to death. Dilar had learned the story by bits and pieces, puzzling over it for hours, for he could not truly understand "cold" and "freezing."

He had determined that this winter Dorna and Norna would not lack for firewood, would not have to go out into the snow, whatever snow was. He had started making a neat stack of dry branches and logs close to the house. Norna had been at first taken aback and even a little scornful, but she had at last agreed that it might not be such a bad notion. And Dorna had even added to the pile, though most of the wood she brought was half-rotted bits which crumbled before she got them home.

There was now enough wood to last most of the short winter, Dilar felt. They would not have to search in the snow. But he went out to gather more. There might be some emergency; Grandfather was always expecting an emergency as he put away more dried fish. In his heart Dilar knew that he was not preparing for an emergency but putting off the day when he must make a final decision about leaving. So he counted himself lucky to come right away upon two fallen trees. Now he would be too busy hacking up the trees and taking them home to think very much.

He was struggling along the path toward Norna's house, dragging a log, when he met Katran, walking beside a donkey. Katran stared at the log and then at Dilar, but he said nothing. He nodded to Dilar and passed him by, but in a few minutes Dilar heard him coming back.

"I could wonder if a donkey might not carry that more easily," he said, staring at a point beside Dilar's left ear. Dilar grinned. "Perhaps," he answered, "but I haven't a donkey."

"Why, here is a donkey," said Katran, sounding a little surprised. "You could make use of it."

"But then you would not be able to use it," Dilar pointed out.

Katran shrugged. "I am not using it. I am taking it to the mountain meadow so it will be ready early tomorrow when we leave." He looked directly at Dilar for the first time and for a minute seemed to be enjoying the boy's puzzlement, and his struggle not to ask questions. Then he smiled.

"We will go up the Mountains of the Tigers to the Place of Stones. We take many donkeys to carry stones and with them we barricade the passes the tigers use. We don't like to have the tigers come down into the valley. Especially not in winter. They've been known to kill sheep and donkeys and even men during the time of the snows."

He hesitated a minute. "It is hard work," he added. "You're welcome to come along, for young, strong, willing workers are always needed. We meet at the foot of the mountain meadow tomorrow at sunup."

Dilar gazed up at those great peaks, already stained and streaked with white which Dorna said was snow. Dilar wanted to see snow. He had waited for something to tell him where and when to go. Now this seemed to be what he had been waiting for. "I will be there," he told Katran. "I will be there at sunup."

Norna was disapproving. "It is a thing for the People Against the Tigers to do, not you," she said, and it gave Dilar a pang. Even Norna still felt his strangeness. Even she would never treat him as one of them.

Dorna said, "Katran should have warned you, it is

cold, cold, cold, in the mountains. Even in summer the mountains are cold at night."

This made Norna laugh. "Dorna is a hug-the-hearth all winter," she told Dilar. "She cannot bear the least chill. It is not that bad in the mountains. Besides I have clothes that will keep you warm, things that once were my husband's. I have them as a sort of keepsake, though I should have given them away long ago." She shook her head, thinking of Katran's boldness. "If you are determined to go you shall have them."

Out of a chest she took a jacket, leggings, a cap, and a sort of cape that could serve also as a blanket. She pressed them on him. "Take them," she urged. "You'll need them. And see, they are going to waste here. The crickets have already been chewing on the leggings."

Dilar took them. He was leaving. He was going. That night he could not sleep.

In the morning Norna gave him a packet of cakes, and she and Dorna bade him farewell.

"Take care," said Norna, looking at him gravely, and then kissed him suddenly on the forehead.

"Perhaps we can go dancing when you come back," said Dorna in a wistful voice. They suspected he did not mean to return to them, he thought, and was filled with sorrow and fear at the thought of leaving them. He could not speak, but only waved his hand to them as he walked off toward the mountain meadow.

It was a day's long journey to the Place of Stones, for the little donkeys walked slowly. The boys and young men with whom Dilar traveled grew impatient, ran ahead, played games, raced, shouted, and sang. Dilar joined in the fun, but though the others were kind to him, called his name, challenged him to race, he felt more than ever that he was a stranger. Of the others even the youngest boys who had never been on this mission before knew the trail, knew where they were headed and what to do when they got there.

But more than that it was something in himself, he knew, that would not let him forget the strange place he came from, so strange that these people could not dream of what it was like or believe him if he told them.

The Place of Stones was halfway up the mountainside, a great hollow in the cliffs where centuries ago some natural accident had shaken loose a great rubble of stones and left the walls so broken and shattered that more kept falling.

They reached their destination just as the sun was slipping out of the sky. Dilar found that Dorna was right. If what he was was cold, he was very cold, and he didn't care much for it. He wrapped his blanket around him and when fires were built he came close to warm himself.

That night, while they ate, the men sang songs and told stories. Dilar was fascinated. On the rafts no one told stories and though Norna and Dorna had occasionally told him some tale, he had never before heard anything like these. Tales of riches and power and strangenesses. The ones that interested Dilar the most were the stories that dealt in magic, especially spells and curses. Were the People of the Rafts under a curse? Had they done some evil thing in the past and been condemned to atone for it? And was he—his heart quailed—the one chosen to break the curse and deliver them? Was that why he had so many weeks ago stepped from the raft onto the stone ledge?

He woke during the night and thought about it again and gave a little shiver. He hoped it was not so. He didn't think he was very brave or able to do many daring deeds.

In the morning the work began. It was the boys' task to fill the donkeys' baskets with stones. The men climbed the mountain to repair the barricades that closed the passes. As always, it astonished Dilar that the people could work so hard and well and long. Lifting the stones and filling the baskets was a back-breaking task but none of the boys grumbled; they hardly paused long enough to eat.

On the third day Katran, leading two donkeys, came up to the place where Dilar worked with three other boys loading the baskets with rocks. "Today I will go to the highest pass," he said. "Come with me to see the high mountains. You can help with my work today, for the work here is nearly done and you won't be needed."

Dilar turned to the other boys. "Is that all right?" he asked. "Will you mind if I go?"

The others looked surprised and the oldest boy even laughed. "Go ahead!" he said. "Whether you work here or there or don't work at all doesn't make that much difference. Things will get done sooner or later. You have been a help to us. Still if you had not been here at all the baskets would have got filled. Isn't that so, Katran?"

Katran nodded and laughed too. Dilar almost laughed himself. He should have known how it was. On the rafts if there was some work that required all the men to work together each was expected to do his share. Here, all that was asked was that the thing be done and done it somehow always was. He still could not get used to the difference.

He was glad to stop all the eternal stooping and bending and carrying and walk beside Katran and the donkeys, and he had hoped for a chance such as this all along. He gazed around him with amazement, having come once again into a new and strange world.

The snow gleamed on the slopes above them, the air thinned and chilled, the sky hung just over the mountaintops. The climbing, climbing cliffs, the stunted, squatty trees, the dark rocks marked with great ancient circles of lichen seemed to Dilar as foreign as the meadows and byways of the valley had once seemed.

By noon they had reached the pass and sat a few minutes to recover their breath before starting work. "It's easier and quicker going down," said Katran.

The little donkeys grew suddenly restive, kicked about and made their curious noises. Katran looked up and laid his hand on Dilar's arm. "Look! A tiger!" he whispered.

Dilar expected something ugly and fierce the way he always imagined the willimars to be. Now he drew in his breath. The great broad head with gleaming green eyes, the thick fur, cream and black and orange, the slow grace of its movements along the ledge where it walked—he could have watched forever. But the tiger, having glanced at the two men and the donkeys, with sudden lazy elegance flowed down to the ledge below and disappeared among some boulders. "Ah, ah, how beautiful!" cried Dilar. "How beautiful and strange."

"Beautiful and strange," agreed Katran, "but I wish they lived somewhere else."

The pass was narrow and already filled with stones, but Katran and Dilar used the ones they had brought to replace those which had rolled down from the sides or been dislodged one way or another. Katran climbed up and placed another row across the top.

Would such a barrier turn aside a strong creature like a tiger? Dilar wondered. But he did not ask.

"Is this as far as anyone can go?" he asked instead, forgetting that it was not good manners. But Katran did not seem to mind. "How far one goes depends on where one wants to go. If you want to go beyond this pass you have only to climb over and go." He shrugged a little. "It is said that people go. It is said that people live in the mountains and in the lands beyond, for people live everywhere. To get there perhaps they climbed beyond this pass."

He paused and squinted up at the slopes. "I have heard that people who seek things or people who have some kind of trouble go over the mountains. As for me, if I went there I think I would only want to come home. Here the meadows are bright enough and the fruits sweet enough to suit me." He shook his head thinking about these things and then he said, "But though I have heard of many people going over the mountains, I have never heard of one coming back."

Dilar did not answer. They finished placing all the stones and then began the descent. When they had walked for nearly an hour, Dilar said to Katran, "I have left my cap at the pass. I must go back."

"I'll go with you," offered Katran, and Dilar said, "No, no, I can find the way. The donkeys are eager to get back to the Place of Stones. I can run. It won't take me long."

He turned and started back up the mountainside. He climbed and climbed, and though he did not look back for a long time he was certain that Katran's eyes were on his back.

CHAPTER 7

When he reached the pass Dilar retrieved his cap from behind a rock where he had left it to give himself an excuse for returning. He put it on and stood looking up at the barricade. It would not be easy to climb, but he could do it. He could be on the other side and a good way farther up the mountain before dark.

Also he could turn and hurry down the way he had come and soon be back at the Place of Stones with Borba and Katran and the others. Tomorrow they would be going home and he too could go, back to Norna and Dorna and the little flat-roofed houses and the hens. . . .

He shook his head. No, Norna and Dorna had not invited him to leave the rafts and come into their lives. It had been his own doing and whatever lay ahead of him was something he must attend to by himself. Remembering how he had got off the raft, all at once, swiftly and without debate, he suddenly set his feet on the lowest of the stones and began to search for the easiest way up.

It took him longer to reach the top than he had thought it would, and finding his way down the other side, which was almost sheer, took longer yet. When he finally made his way to the bottom, the light was getting dim. The way led off among great rocks and a few scattered low-growing bushes. It looked menacing and filled with fear. Tigers and worse lurked in the shadows. Dilar was tired. He only went a little way before he decided to stop for the night.

He had no fire. The night was cold, and he had left the others without anything to make fire with. He had watched them often enough, striking two stones together to make a spark that fell into dry grass or rotted wood and set it ablaze. But he did not know the right kinds of rocks to use nor the proper way to strike them together. Now he spent some time trying with two stones that looked like the ones Borba and Norna and the others used. But nothing happened; no spark was struck.

He should have learned to make fire; he should have brought the proper rocks with him. Fire, the others told him, kept the tigers away. And it kept off the cold. He had been no more practical than they. He had not thought of the future and now he would suffer for it.

For food he had only the last crumbs of the cakes Norna had given him. At the Place of Stones there had been enough to eat and more: dried fruits and berries still clinging to bushes and vines, nuts and puffballs and tubers that the others knew how to prepare for eating, as well as the supplies they had brought with them.

But there were none of these things here, Dilar thought. Tomorrow he would have to make a plan for getting some food—fishing in a stream, or trapping birds, or something.

He gathered small branches from the bushes and piled them together to make a bed, fashioned against the western side of a boulder still warm from the sun. The leaves were spicy smelling and soft and though the pallet was not so comfortable as some he had slept on, he was tired from the long day's work. Even the thought of tigers did not keep him awake long.

He awoke, shivering, quaking, colder than he had ever been in his life. The stars showed faintly through a mist of clouds, the moon was setting, and it would be an hour or more till daylight. What had roused him? Just the cold, or had a tiger screamed close by, or even walked near his bed?

The sun's warmth had long since left the stones and the cold seemed to flow from them into his bones. He sat up and wrapped his cloak more tightly about him and crouched among his branches, shaking and shaking. When the sky began to gray and all the tigers around him began to turn into rocks and bushes, he struggled up and set out once more. The way was rough and steep. In the gloom he stumbled and slipped and spent as much time on his hands and knees as on his feet. He had hoped that walking would make him warmer, but he walked and walked and was as cold as ever. The air grew colder and colder. In the rifts of the rocks white pools and drifts of frost and snow appeared, and where water seeped down the cliffsides it was not moisture that his fingers touched but a hard glaze of ice that made his hands ache and his feet slide.

He came on a cliff hung with icicles. In spite of his misery he stopped to admire the long upside-down candles of ice, fluted and twisted and clear. Even winter had its wonders in this strange land.

He waited and watched for the sun—the sun would

make him warmer—but the day was overcast. The clouds grew thicker and seemed to hang almost over his head. Snow began to drop down from the sky, a flake here, a flake there. He did not know what it was, but when a flake fell on his sleeve he stared at its beautiful starry shape till it melted and then he decided it must be snow.

More and more of it fell. It began to pile up on the rocks around him, a thin layer of white on the stones like ashes on the hearth at Norna's house.

He tried to hurry. He would get to the top of the mountain. He did not know why—he was too cold to think—but somehow he felt that if he got to the top things would be better, he would be warmer and safer. He imagined how it would be at the crest of the mountain, sunny, quiet, peaceful. There would still be snow, but it would be warm snow, the sky would be blue and the sun's touch gentle and friendly. There would be a stream full of fish, and shelter under trees. He went over and over these things, to shut out the sight of the cliffs and the precipices and the barrenness.

His heart thumped and fluttered in his chest, his breath came into his lungs like thrusts of a dull knife, his hands and feet scrabbled frantically at the stones and cliffsides. But he was coming closer to his goal, he was coming nearer. Every step up meant he was coming closer, and at last he was there!

He would not have known he was there except that he had stopped climbing. There was no warmth or safety here, only more snow, more rocks, more scruffy ever-green trees bowed down with ice. What foolish things had he been expecting? He stared about dully. The air was hard as iron, he could scarcely breathe, his hands and feet ached with cold. It was all he could do to take one step forward and another. He staggered on between the trees under the heavy sky. The snow was deep, the surface crusted with ice, and it chopped and cut at his ankles.

A branch from a tree close by suddenly snapped and broke with the weight of snow and ice. The sound was huge in the still air and it seemed to wake Dilar from his daze. He raised his head and looked in every direction, but there was nothing to see, no moving thing, no house, no path, no help.

He was going to die then, as Dorna's father had died in the snow looking for firewood. The cold would kill him, and hunger. The tigers would eat his body and that would be the end of him.

On the raft he had never been hungry or cold or afraid. He had not known that it was possible to suffer as he suffered now with cold, with pain in his legs and arms, with grief in his heart. "Grandfather!" he whispered through half-frozen lips.

He went on. There was nothing else to do. He would not stand and let death overtake him; he would go on as far as he could force himself to go. He felt as though his body weighed forty times its natural weight and lifting a foot was the greatest effort. But he went on, slouching from side to side through the snow until at last he fell to his knees and could not get up, could only kneel there and try to keep himself from falling flat.

A kind of numbness stole up his legs. It was death and he recognized its soft and evil touch. It was a sorry way to die. Perhaps it was a sorry reason to die, hoping to prove

to Grandfather that the rafts were going nowhere. . . .
But he would have liked to show Grandfather "green"
and "day." He would have liked, if only for a moment,
to show the Raft People that world they had left.

The snow fell softly. He listened to the tiny sound, like
a little bell. A bell . . . it was water falling. He knew
that ring. It was the sweet dripping of moving water! If
there was water running, then there was someplace nearby where it was warmer, where he could perhaps find
shelter. He started up and gazed around and saw the
smoking stream running through the snow. He gasped
and tried to struggle to his feet. He did not want to die.
He wanted to get away from death and make it lose its
hateful hold on his legs. He pushed himself erect and
floundered over to the water's edge and dipped a finger
into it. Warm, the water was warm to his touch! Why was
it warm? He turned to follow it among the rocks, slipped
and fell once more, but went forward on his knees, pull-
ing himself along by his hands, crawling, creeping, wrig-
gling through the snow.

The rivulet issued from a shallow cave. The rocks
around the entrance were bare of snow and ice, and there
were even some tiny ferns and mosses growing in the
crevices. Dilar crawled nearer, trembling and panting,
and then staggered upright and in a rush flung himself
across the last stretch of snow and into the mouth of the
cave.

The air was so hot it almost pushed him out again. It
felt thick and solid and the smell was acrid. The rocks
underneath him were warm. He hardly knew whether to
believe it or not. How could there be in this place of frost

and snow a little cave full of fire and heat? Perhaps he was out of his mind and making the whole thing up.

Against the back of the cave a spring rose up among the rocks, seething and bubbling as hot water had boiled in one of Norna's pots. Dilar dared not go any nearer. It was so hot in the cave, and he was afraid. He stood just inside the entrance, feeling the warmth creep over him, and glad of it, but still afraid, still not quite believing it, not knowing what would happen next.

His hands and feet began to prickle and tingle and then to ache most horribly. The pain increased quickly and he wrung his hands and jumped up and down, groaning and grunting. It went on and on and he fell down and writhed on the floor of the cave, yelling with pain. It was the melting of the ice in his fingers and toes that made them hurt so, he was sure. He rushed out into the snow and thrust his hands and feet into a drift, hoping to freeze them into numbness again, but it did not help much and the rest of him was so cold, so cold, so cold, and he shook and shook. He ran back to the cave and stood holding his hands out in front of him, wailing like a mad thing, and at last the agony eased and he sat down on the warm floor, rocking back and forth, moaning every now and then, and fell asleep.

When he woke he was confused, for he had been dreaming about the rafts and here he was lying in darkness with a watch fire glowing red beside him. Then he got a whiff of the pungent smell and he knew immediately where he was. Night had come for there was only that strange glow from the spring. It was silent except for the spring's warm, bubbly chuckle and the high-voiced singing of the cold outside the cave. Dilar's hands stung and burned.

He started to rub them together, but he did not. Something told him suddenly not to move, to lie as still as he could and breathe only the least breath he could breathe. Something was moving about in the cave, roaming around him, something big. He could smell its wild, wild smell as it came close. He could hear its rasping purr. He did not have to see it to know what it was—a tiger!

CHAPTER 8

The tiger came closer—pad, pad, pad, on its great feet. Its hot breath blew along his cheek. Dilar's own breath stuck in his chest somewhere and swelled and swelled till his ears rang and red flashes appeared before his eyes. But he did not move. Even if the tiger opened its great jaws and sank its teeth into his throat he would just have to lie there and be eaten, for he could not move. The tiger's whiskers and cold nose touched his ear.

Then it was gone. Still Dilar did not move. He lay feeling the sweat run down his ribs and his breath slowly whispered and trickled out of his lungs. And then before he could fill his chest again the tiger came running back. It flung itself down beside him and he could hear it rolling back and forth on the cave floor, making little growling noises. Once its tail flipped across his face and twice a big paw grazed along his back. Finally the tiger sighed, a whooshing meat-tainted sigh, and then was motionless and quiet.

Dilar was almost too frightened to think. He knew the tiger was right behind him. He thought it was asleep, but he dared not turn over to find out. He listened to its breathing, a deep grating, puffing in and out, but he did not know whether that was the sound of a tiger snoring or not. He lay watching the dim glow at the back of the cave and thinking that in a minute he would summon up his courage and roll over and face the tiger. If it killed him that would be all right. What did he have to live for —he who had left his proper home for a reason he could not understand himself and who could not find his way back? Nowhere in this strange new world was there a place for him. Besides, being eaten by a tiger might be quicker and less painful than dying of cold and hunger. In a minute he would spring at the tiger and it would kill him. . . .

Then the tiger yawned loudly and rose to its feet. Once again Dilar froze. He remembered that he did not after all want to die, and especially he did not want to die of being eaten by a tiger. Once more the tiger's huge head leaned over him and this time it growled suddenly and seemed to crouch and bend forward as though to swallow him whole.

Things happened all at once: a stir and rattle at the back of the cave, a cry of fear and agony from Dilar, and a startled cough from the tiger. "Get along, get along now," cried a man's voice, and the tiger growled again and suddenly swirled about so that once more its tail struck Dilar and then it was gone. Dilar, though he was nearly fainting, jumped to his feet and leaped toward the back of the cave. Someone was there, someone who had helped him. Another human being!

The man at the back of the cave was huge. It was not that he was so much taller than average, but that he was broader, with great wide shoulders, and thicker, with a big belly, and big hands and feet and a face as wide as a plate. He seemed stunned by the sight of Dilar and stood holding a wooden bucket and letting his mouth hang open.

"Well, young cub," he said at last, "well, well, did the tiger drag you here? Are you hurt? Are you bit?"

"No, no," gasped Dilar. "You saved me. I would have been eaten, but you saved me."

"Saved!" The big man looked astonished. Then he laughed. "Oh, I doubt the tiger would have hurt you. Still maybe you're right. I saved you. Oh, it gladdens my heart to think so and it's a lucky day all around, for company's a thing that's very rare for me. Now wait a bit and I'll fetch some water and we'll talk."

He walked to the front of the cave and glanced quickly out into a wan dawnlight. Then he scooped up a great bucketful of icy snow and came back to Dilar. "This way," he said, and there among the rocks was a door, a wooden door so narrow that Dilar wondered that the man could get through. He pushed it open and squeezed in and held it for Dilar. On the other side was a much bigger cave, only it wasn't like a cave at all. A great fire blazed at one end, a bed and a cupboard and chairs stood against the walls, a table in front of the fire, and bright rugs covered the floor and even hung on the walls.

"Now, that's a surprise, eh?" said the big man with a chuckle. "Turn about's fair play, for you surprised me, you really did."

He set the bucket down by the fire and began to fuss about among the ashes. By and by he drew some smoking cakes out of a stone oven. "Sit down and make yourself comfortable and we'll eat. A good hot breakfast makes the day, I say."

There were eggs, too, and wonderful-smelling bacon and a sort of hot drink and bowls of cooked fruit. Dilar was starving and with his itching, burning hands he stuffed himself with all these delicious things. The man kept on smiling and talking and bringing more and more of the cakes from his oven.

"Have some peaches. Oh, they have a flavor like the sun peeking out on a gray day. I brought them up from the slopes last summer, eight basketloads of them. Such a hot day." He sighed and rubbed his head, remembering the heat. Then he chuckled. "But I knew it would be worth it and it was. Now these cakes are made of the finest oats. I don't know how many miles I traveled to find them, but don't they make good cakes? The best is none too good, and I do always try to get the best. Have some pears. They are stewed in clover honey, the very sweetest honey. . . ."

He never seemed to stop talking and while he talked he ate. Dilar ate plenty but he had no idea anyone could eat as much as the big man ate—acres of hot cakes and bacon, barrels of berries and peaches, egg after egg. And still there was more, still he drew cakes and cakes and cakes out of the oven and set them to cool.

"My name's Wingo," he said suddenly. "Have another cake."

"I am called Dilar," said Dilar. "No more cakes."

He was going to add that he was one of the Raft People and that he had been living among the People Against the Tigers. But Wingo suddenly swooped up a little bowl of warm grease from the hearth and seized Dilar's hands and began to rub the grease into his frost-bitten fingers. "We'll do this every so often and those places will soon heal," he explained. "It happens to me once in a while and this is the best remedy. We don't want them to give you any trouble, for we have a lot of work to do, oh, a lot, and sore fingers might interfere. Now come along, boy, and I'll show you what must be done."

From one corner of the cave he fetched an enormous bowl and set it on the table. Then he strode over and opened a door near the bed and beckoned Dilar to follow. Another cave, this one filled with boxes and barrels and bins, hung with hams and strings of onions and net bags full of fruits and vegetables. Dilar was amazed to find that there was so much to eat in the world.

With Dilar's help Wingo carried a big sack of oatmeal, many eggs, and a jug of oil into the other room. He soon had another lot of cakes baking in his oven. He picked up a great basket and filled it with cooled cakes.

"Now here we go!" cried Wingo, and opened the door through which he and Dilar had first entered. He shouted and stamped his feet as he peered around, looking for tigers.

"They come in here once in a while," he explained. "But they always run when I holler. It may be they think a man my size might make more breakfast than even a tiger would want. Now you, you'll have to be more careful." He chuckled and Dilar smiled, though he remembered too clearly the tiger's purring voice in his ear to think such things were very funny.

He followed Wingo out into the snow. Was the big man just going to throw the cakes away? Why make such a huge number of them if all he did was dump them in the snow?

After the heat of the caves the cold seemed worse than ever to Dilar and he hoped, whatever their errand, it was soon over. Wingo walked steadily along through the trees. They were fairly large, about half of them needled evergreens, others bare-branched, silver-barked trees with long, dried seed pods trailing from the twigs. A bird, pecking at one of these pods, gave a sharp cry at the sight of the two of them and suddenly the trees were filled with birds, blue and red and black, birds with spotted wings and tails, birds with crowns and crests and plumes, calling and whistling and singing.

In a little clearing Wingo stopped and put down his basket. He took up some of the cakes and crumbled them in his hands and threw the pieces onto the hard snow. The birds flocked down to eat. Almost before the crumbs left his hands they were crowding around him, lighting on his arms and head and shoulders, snatching the bread from his fingers.

"Now, now, little friends, don't be so greedy," he said softly, chuckling, and reached for more cakes. Squirrels came running up for their share and Dilar glimpsed other animals in the undergrowth. He picked up a cake and tossed it in among the bushes and saw little creatures scurrying away from it, then coming cautiously back to nibble at the food.

"Oh, it does my heart good!" cried Wingo when the basket was empty and the bread all scattered on the ground. "Come along, boy, more work to do."

Twice more they filled the basket and carried it to different places in the woods. Dilar watched while Wingo put cakes in the oven and took them out, then shivered

67

along behind as Wingo bore the basket through the snow, and sometimes tossed a cake or two to the birds and squirrels. He thought it was the least work he'd ever done. But Wingo seemed to think he was working and kept urging him to eat one of the oat cakes to keep his strength up. He seemed overjoyed at having Dilar with him and talked and talked and talked. Back at the caves he showed Dilar all his storerooms, the ones that were warmed by air from the hot springs and the ones that were cooled by freezing drafts from outside. He told where he got these supplies and how he ground the flours and meals himself, and dried the fruits, and stored the eggs. He talked without stopping while he cooked and baked and scrubbed the bowls and spoons and swept up the spills on the floor. Dilar tried to help, but beyond fetching and carrying there was not much he could do.

Still, listening proved to be tiring and by the time he had eaten his bowl of soup and made a pallet on the floor before the fire from the robes and blankets supplied by Wingo, he was so weary he fell asleep almost before he stretched out.

Only when he woke the next morning and heard Wingo stirring in his big bed did he begin to think. Was this the wise man he was looking for, this generous, cheerful, kindhearted man? He was surely wiser than Borba and Fortan and Katran, for though he lived here in the mountains where the winters were longer and harder than in the valley, he had prepared for them well. A man who spent all his life looking after birds and animals and singing and chuckling must be a happy man, must know some secrets. Was he the one who could tell Dilar the answers to his questions?

CHAPTER 9

Afterward Dilar could not remember how long he stayed with Wingo. The days went by, each one very like the other, warm and bright, filled with the good smells of baking and cooking, and the sound of Wingo talking and talking and talking. Every day he cooked their meals and made his basketloads of cakes and tended his stores. Dilar helped and soon learned to do it all himself by watching. But Wingo would only let him do the simplest things— stir the soup occasionally or fetch things from the store-rooms or sweep the floors.

"It takes a clever hand to feed the fire for baking," he'd say. "And you might get burned." Or: "No, no, you have to know just how long to beat in the eggs for good cakes, and the batter's heavy, it might strain your arm to beat it." Or: "Let me lift that bag. A young fellow like you hasn't the strength."

Dilar might have been bored with so little to do except that Wingo talked so much, told so many stories, sang so many songs. He knew about every bag of meal and every bowl of honey in his pantries and could tell a tale about each one. Dilar was the best of listeners, for almost everything was new to him, a boy of the Raft People. And besides he kept hoping to learn more about Wingo by listening to him, to discover whether this really was a wise man who knew the answers to all questions.

Not that Wingo ever let him ask a question or listened to him when he said anything. "I am one of the Raft People," Dilar said carefully one day as Wingo was putting a panful of cakes into his oven.

"Are you now?" answered Wingo. "Did I tell about the time I brought a load of grapes up the mountain on a donkey? I had to spend the night on the mountainside and in the night the donkey ate all the grapes. Every one!" He laughed till the tears came to his eyes.

"Once I went to trade some meal for oil with a man who lived on a river," he began another day, and Dilar interrupted quickly, "I am one of the Raft People and I used to live on a river. I spent my whole life on a raft."

"I suppose it was more of a lake than a river," said Wingo vaguely. "A good, big lake with oil nut trees growing all around. He had a kind of mill to press the oil out of the nuts, and it ran down a little stone trough into a stone vat, the best and clearest oil I ever saw. I've got some now, in the cold rooms. . . ."

"Don't you want to hear about where I came from?" cried Dilar once impatiently, and Wingo said in some surprise, "Why certainly I do, I'm listening. Not that it makes any difference where you come from. You are here, and that's what matters. It is right now that is important, I always say. And it is, you know. Hand me that pan and we'll have these cakes in the oven in no time." And he began to stir and beat the dough with such a clatter that Dilar could only fall silent and watch.

Three days after Dilar's arrival it began to snow

heavily. The snow fell and fell, piling up in great, soft drifts that delighted Dilar's eyes, heaping up along the branches of the trees, covering the rocks till the world stretched away from the cave door smoothly white, shadowed and hollowed with greens and blues and lavenders that made Dilar's heart ache for reasons he could not name.

Wingo was busier than ever, his baking was frantic. When they went out to carry the basketloads of cakes into the woods, he showed Dilar how to walk in the snow, to follow the sheltered side of evergreens and the paths made by the larger animals. For a long way they went through an arched passage where branches grew close and the snow caught among them to make a sort of roof over the space between the trees. Dilar did not like walking in this white, silent, low-ceilinged tunnel. It made him feel shut away and unhappy. He could not go back to the rafts ever, he thought suddenly. He would never learn again to live in so narrow and confined a place.

Wingo hurried through the drifts and along the paths. He huffed and puffed and panted, sweat sprang up on his forehead as they struggled through the snow. "I try to get to the feeding places before the cakes get cold," he gasped out to Dilar. "Oh, my poor little creatures, they need warm food in weather like this. Oh, their poor little feet in the snow!"

"Let me carry the basket," pleaded Dilar. "It is easier for me. I am strong. Let me carry the basket."

"No, no," answered Wingo breathlessly. "It's too heavy. Anyway, all I can do for my little friends is to bring them their warm cakes."

So they floundered on, Dilar hopping ahead, for by this time he knew the route well. It was useless trying to make the way easier for Wingo, however, for Dilar was only half his weight. Icy crust that merely bent and squeaked under Dilar's feet gave way entirely under the big man's step and made his going even harder than before.

After the snowfall the cold was bitterer than ever. The sun came out and made the world a blaze of blue-white light, the air sparkled with ice crystals floating in the sun beams. "Even the air is frozen," Dilar thought. Cold was nothing like what he had imagined. It did not, like heat, press against you, hover around you; instead it pulled and tore at you with narrow, pinching fingers. He wondered what other strange things there were in the world. Was there any way to be besides cold and hot, and what could those other ways be? Would he ever find out? Should he leave here to find out? Or should he stay with Wingo? Perhaps when the snow went away Wingo would have time to stop and think a minute and answer a question or two. . . .

He did not believe anyway that he wanted to leave now in this cold. Sometimes he wondered about Dorna and Norna and Borba and the others, hungry, shivering in their ill-heated houses. He told himself that Dorna was right and that cold was a terrible thing. And yet it was beautiful. He could not help admiring the snow, the sun twinkling on the ice-bent trees, the strange echoless sounds in the wrapped and muffled world, the flash of a bird among the immaculate tree branches. And when twilight swept over the mountaintop it made tears come to his eyes, it was so lovely and sad.

Since the snow there were tigers in the warm outer cave almost every time Dilar and Wingo went out. Wingo shouted and beat on the walls with a metal bar and they always got up lazily and drifted outside. How handsome and bright they were in the snow! When the crust was soft and they broke through and thrashed about in the cold white stuff, their movements were so lithe and their colors so brilliant that sometimes Dilar ran to the front of the cave to watch them out of sight.

"Be careful! Be careful!" warned Wingo. "They'll chew you into splinters and mud. They're treacherous."

But to Dilar they did not seem anxious even to turn back and look at him. How sleek they were! They looked lazy and content, as though all they asked for was a warm place to lie down and stretch.

More snow fell, and more; drifts piled upon drifts until in some places the trees were half buried. Every morning there was a new skin of snow over yesterday's fall. It almost hid things that worried Dilar a great deal but which Wingo seemed not to notice, things that Dilar termed to himself "the bloody places": spots in the snow where some creature had died a violent death, blood on the broken crust, sad little heaps of bone and fur or feathers. Dilar never mentioned them to Wingo, for he knew the big man must mourn the death of each of his small friends, each of the little beasts he worked so hard to care for every day.

"How long does the winter last here on the mountains?" Dilar asked one morning as he stood hugging himself to keep out the cold, waiting for Wingo to empty his basket.

"A long time," said Wingo with a chuckle. "And when

it is done the work begins. Oh, you and I will be busy indeed then, my young friend. As soon as the bees swarm in the valley and the oil nuts are thoroughly warmed, we have to start our work, we have to begin replenishing our stores."

"You and I," thought Dilar. "*We* have to begin." Did he really want to stay here with Wingo after the cold weather? Was Wingo truly going to be willing then to listen to what he had to say and tell him what to do? If he was going to be busier than ever, would he have even a minute to stop and listen to Dilar?

Later he wandered away from Wingo and climbed through the drifted snow, pondering. He had to stay here until the snow stopped and the weather warmed, he knew. But longer than that?

His head was almost on a level with the first branches of a tall tree. When the snow melted those branches would be far out of his reach. He grabbed one suddenly and swung himself up and climbed quickly to a point where he could look down on Wingo and the flocks of birds.

After a minute he realized that he was not the only one watching. In the needled evergreen tree next to him another pair of eyes was fastened on the feeding birds, with the eager, unwavering gaze of the hunter. Dilar drew in his breath, watching that proud head with its fierce, dark sideburns and its strong, tearing beak. It would be useless, he knew, to try to warn the smaller birds or to frighten the hawk away. Sooner or later, while the birds were bemused with warm crumbs, those sharp talons would find their mark.

Slowly Dilar descended his tree and slid and slithered down the snowbanks to the path that he and Wingo had trod to the feeding place. When he got to that spot, Wingo had emptied the basket and stood holding the last piece of cake in his hand while a little green bird sat on his thumb and pecked contentedly as Wingo spoke to it softly.

"Now where have you been?" cried Wingo cheerfully. "We must hurry. There'll be storms again this afternoon. We won't be able to go out. We'll have to sit by the fire and I'll make a special plum and honey cake and I'll tell you a tale about how I caught the great long-legged blue bird of the lakes and made him work for me." He chuckled at the thought and then added hastily, "I didn't make him work very hard, of course."

It was a pleasant prospect, Dilar thought, to sit warm and snug and eating the fragrant cake while Wingo talked and talked. But was this how he wanted to spend his life, forever and ever? Was this how he was going to find the answers to his questions?

They walked through the snow and Dilar looked back to see the hawk crouched in the top of the tree, all its body tensed and aimed, like an arrow drawn back in the bowstring.

"Look," he said to Wingo. "Look at the hawk in the top of that tree."

Wingo turned his head. "Where?" he asked.

"There, in the top of the evergreen tree." Dilar pointed.

Wingo stared and then shook his head. "Your eyes are playing tricks on you," he said at last. "There aren't any hawks on this mountain." And he hurried on.

Dilar followed. But he had new questions to fret over now. Was Wingo really a man of kindliness and wisdom? Or was it stupid and cruel to lure birds and animals to places where they were easy victims? No wonder the tigers were so sleek and slow to rouse, with nothing to do but wait for Wingo to provide dinner for them as he provided it for the birds. Thinking about it made Dilar's flesh creep a little. Didn't Wingo know what happened? Didn't he see the bloody places in the snow? What was the matter with his eyes that kept him from seeing the hawk?

The snowstorms did come before they could fill the basket and carry it outside once more. Wingo was distressed but soon busied himself making the plum and honey cake and telling Dilar the story he had promised. Dilar sat gazing into the fire hardly hearing the words. No, he told himself, Wingo could not be a wise man. He did not answer questions, only filled Dilar's mind with new and different ones.

"Wingo," he said suddenly, "I must leave this place. I must travel on from here."

There was a moment's astonished silence and then the big man cried, "How can you say such a thing? You don't mean what you say? No, no, you wouldn't leave me. Who would help me carry the cakes? Who would help me bake? Who would keep me company?" His voice rose to a loud and desperate note.

Dilar smiled a little uneasily. "I don't help you, Wingo," he said. "You could get along without me just as you did before I came. And for company, you've got the birds and animals. They are your friends and always will be."

A crafty, almost mean look stole over Wingo's face. "Anyway," he said, "you can't leave now, in the snow, in the cold. How would you keep warm and fed if you left here? You must wait till warmer days anyway."

And he thrust a great, smoking buttery piece of the cake at Dilar and began once again to tell his story.

But Dilar could hardly swallow a mouthful. Suddenly he was frightened. Like the birds and the little animals, had Wingo's cakes and warm fires lured him into some kind of trap where something waited to fall on him and tear him to bits? Was he to be a victim too?

In the next few days Wingo was as jolly as ever. Still he seemed to Dilar to keep a watchful eye on him all the time. He let Dilar do more of the basket carrying and cake crumbling and throwing, so that the boy would not have the opportunity to wander off. He worked harder than ever at telling stories and singing songs; he baked more cakes and made sweetmeats, and every now and then he would pat Dilar's shoulder and tell him what a help he was and how lonely it had been on the mountain-top before he came. Dilar always remembered to thank Wingo for saving his life and say how grateful he was for a place to stay during the cold weather.

Yet the cold weather was going. Snow fell, but the hard crust began to disappear. Wading through the slushy wet stuff was uncomfortable, and the places on Dilar's feet where the frost had bitten him so many weeks ago burned and stung. He and Wingo hurried back to the fire after taking out each load of cakes, and sometimes Dilar's clothes were still damp and clammy by the time the next basketful was ready. Wingo was right. He must certainly wait for warmer weather.

Still he told himself he could lay plans. Even under Wingo's constant surveillance he could lay plans and make ready to go. He knew which way he should travel, and as they walked in that direction he often noted land-marks and lines of trees and shelter against rocks where the going would be easiest and quickest. Once he found the edge of the mountain, the way down into the valley would be simple. He had climbed up and doubtless he could climb down.

He began to long to go, to be more eager than he had ever been before to leave the blazing hearth and Wingo's constant talk and all the urging to eat "just one more cake." Every day he looked for more signs that the snow was going away.

Perhaps it would never go away, he thought gloomily one night as he lay on his pallet. Perhaps Wingo was only deceiving him, saying the snow and cold would end. Perhaps from now on this was all there would ever be.

He resolved suddenly to leave this very night—to get up in the gleam of the fire and dress, as he had planned to do—wrap himself as warmly as possible, take the pile of food that was always on the table in case Wingo should feel hungry in the night, and slip away to the mountain's rim and back to Norna's house.

Wingo snored on. Quietly, quietly Dilar stood up and put on all the clothes he possessed. He went over to the table and filled his cap with food, since his head and neck were now covered with a warm woolen scarf that Wingo had given him. On tiptoe he walked over to the fire, looked once around the cheerful room, and wished it would be possible to say good-by to Wingo. Then he moved to the door of the cave. He put out his hand and touched the door, which he had never opened himself in all the time he had been there.

He did not even tug on the latch to know that it was useless. The door was too heavy and too firmly wedged into the rock for him to budge. He was a prisoner, as firmly locked inside the cave as he would have been in an iron-barred cage.

CHAPTER 10

Wingo tossed the last crumbs out upon the snow. "Ah, boy, you look gloomy these days," he scolded. "No need to look gloomy. See our friends the birds, how cheerful they are in spite of the cold and snow."

Dilar frowned. "I am not a bird," he said distinctly. "I am a boy. Crumbs are not enough to make me cheerful."

"That may be so," Wingo agreed. "Still better crumbs than hunger, in the days of winter. Besides winter will soon be over."

"No, it won't," responded Dilar darkly. "It will go on forever."

Wingo laughed and shook his head. "Spring is on the way. Come, I'll show you."

He began to walk through the trees, going off toward the morning sun, a way he and Dilar had never ventured before. Dilar followed eagerly. He longed for something different to happen, something besides baking and eating and feeding the birds. And perhaps Wingo would really show him some signs of coming spring. In spite of himself Dilar could not get over the notion that the snow and cold were endless and unchanging.

They walked in snow almost unmarked except by an

occasional track of slender hoofed feet or the brush of a big wing. Dilar wanted to ask Wingo how he found his way so easily, for the big man did not hesitate but went forward swiftly and for once hardly spoke.

"There, now, there it is!" exclaimed Wingo at length and Dilar looked around, not knowing what to expect and not seeing anything except the snowy landscape. But Wingo hurried forward and Dilar followed and to his surprise they stood suddenly on the mountain's edge, at the top of a long, steep slope, looking down into that valley Dilar had never hoped to see, the one beyond the Mountains of the Tigers!

What lay below them was a curiously colored, gently moving mist, but somewhere across the fog, low hills shouldered into view. "See!" cried Wingo, pointing. "The hills are bare of snow. There's even a little green on the slopes, can you see?"

Dilar shaded his eyes with his hands. He thought he saw. He wanted to see. He leaned forward trying hard to see, and then suddenly, horribly, sickeningly, his feet were sliding, he was slipping, he gasped and flung out his arms and laid hold of nothing and saw the world whirl round him, and then was rolling, spinning, slithering straight down the mountain!

He was hurled against a rock and then over a small ledge, landed jarringly on the soft snow beneath and sledded swiftly over it, bounced into a stunted bush and grabbed for it frantically as the twigs broke in his fingers, rolled again down and down and down, and fell over another ledge, scratching and clawing to save himself from going over, trying desperately to slow himself, but vainly, nothing offered itself to his hands and he dropped, gasping, half fainting, into empty space. . . .

He plunged into the snow as into the river and it closed over his head, over his eyes, over his open mouth. He thrashed around in it, striking out as though he were truly swimming, and his feet struck the bottom and he thought quite clearly, The snow kept me from being killed, for he had landed almost gently. But it would kill him if he stayed in it, drown him, smother him, freeze him. He was already buried, entombed in snow. By frenzied kicking and flopping about at last he touched something solid and pulled himself up out of the snow-filled hole into which he had fallen and onto a wide rock shelf where the snow was only ankle deep. He lay in it, taking great sobbing breaths, still seeing stars and snow flash before his eyes, hardly able to focus on the world around him, a dim, unreal place in its steadiness.

Presently his sight cleared and the sound of his own panting grew less and he could, in the silence, suddenly hear Wingo's great voice, bellowing from far above him: "Dilar! Boy! Dilar! Are you there? Can you hear me?"

Dilar sat up and pressed his hands to his head, but he could not answer. To save his life he could not squeeze any sort of noise out of his chest. With trembling hands he untied Wingo's scarf from around his throat and chin. It was a bright scarf, a warm red-brown, and he waved it feebly a few times.

Wingo continued calling, and after a bit Dilar waved the scarf again and then spread it out on the snow where he hoped it could be seen.

"I see you, boy!" cried Wingo then. "I see you. Don't

move now. I'll fetch a rope and pull you up. Just sit there and take care. I won't be long."

Dilar huddled in the snow, waiting. He ached from head to foot, he was bruised and scraped and scuffed all over, his arms felt as though they had been half pulled from their sockets, and his head ached piercingly. It would be a long time before Wingo returned, he knew. It was several miles to the cave, and then another several back to the mountain's edge. Dilar could not help thinking that he would die before the big man brought the rope.

He picked up a handful of snow and pressed it to the knot on his forehead. After a while he felt better. He wasn't really hurt, only jolted and scratched. The sun had come out and shone warmly on his back, calming and comforting him.

He stood up and carefully stretched and flexed his arms and legs. He was surprised to find that they worked as well as ever. He moved around on the ledge, rubbing a bruise here and there, and suddenly smiling a little as he pictured himself plunging down the cliffs. He remembered how Katran had said that going down the mountain was quicker than going up and he wondered if this was what he had meant.

The ledge on which he stood was a fairly wide one. In the clean snow along its rim ran the sharp little tracks of an antelope. They vanished abruptly, as though the antelope had leaped into space, and Dilar went to look. At that spot a steep path wound away below him and the antelope had evidently descended on it. For several minutes Dilar stood following the tracks with his eyes until they disappeared; and below that point was the strange fog filling the valley.

Dilar peered into it for a space. Suddenly he turned around and picked up the scarf. And then he said softly, "Good-by, Wingo," and set his feet where the antelope's hoofs had marked the way.

He slid and slipped but did not fall. Going carefully, putting his feet down slowly, crouching where the drop seemed steeper than he could manage standing, he journeyed down the slopes. Once he turned his head and looked back the way he had come, but the sun on the snow dazzled him and he had to turn his eyes away. But the snow around him was disappearing, rocks and dried grasses and weeds poked up through the thin skin of snow. Only in cracks between the rocks and in occasional hollows was it any longer drifted deep. Before he had been scrambling downward another hour the path itself was clear, and there lay before him a narrow, rough, pebbly way.

As he went on the day grew dim. At first he thought the sun was setting for he did not really know how long he had been going down and down. Then he saw he had reached the level of the mist, that he was descending into those curious clouds, dull blue and brass and copper and brown, gray and lavender and maroon, slowly boiling and twisting and writhing in long ropes and dissolving into pools and erupting into fat, spreading columns. Dilar glanced up and found he could not see the sun and the mountains. Yet the haze around him was not as thick and blinding as it had appeared to be from the mountain's face. He could see things ahead of him easily enough, as if he were walking through a stormy twilight. He stopped to take off the cape that Norna had given him, for he was growing warm in it, and he realized that there was no trace of snow anywhere around him. The ground still went downward but very gradually, the pebbles had changed to smooth sand, and there was nothing to see in all that opalescent mist except here and there a big boulder looming through it. The haze, drifting and spiraling in the little restless winds, now thick, now thin, now blue, now brown, made distances hard to judge; near things were suddenly far away, and distant rocks were in two steps close enough to touch.

It was a strange landscape even to Dilar, and he hesitated. Perhaps he should have thought twice before leaving Wingo and his pantries and his baking. Perhaps there was another way off the mountain which ended somewhere else, a place different from this eerie region of no shadows and no light, no trees, no animals, no people, only the formless murk and the glossless, shifting colors.

It was useless to think of going back. He did not now believe he could retrace his steps and find his way once again up the mountain. What lay behind him was as dim and unmarked as what lay in front. Anyway he had begun to feel that going back would be a mistake, that whatever happened he had to go on until he found whatever it was he was seeking. He was glad that he had not, after all, turned back to Norna's house.

He went on. The earth flattened and grew more sandy, there was no indication of a path. The winds picked up the fine dust and blew it this way and that. Looking up

Dilar found no sun, no moon, no clouds, no stars. He stumbled on. He passed some curious lumpy things, like plants, covered with thin, sharp thorns. A lizard as long as his arm ran in front of him and several times he heard what he thought must be animals barking fairly close to him and once a bird of some sort croaked strangely overhead. All these things, queer and dry and alien as they were, made Dilar feel a little better, for even a lizard for company was better than thinking himself alone, the only living creature in a mysterious dead world.

He was tired and hungry and thirsty but he did not know any remedy for his discomforts and plodded on, mile after mile. It had now grown so dim that he assumed it was night. He looked about him and saw only rocks and the dumpy plants and drifts of sand, just as he had seen them now for hours. He might as well have been walking in circles, for nothing changed except the wash of color through the mists, blues chasing grays chasing reds in a thin film that his eyes could barely catch. Everywhere he looked it was the same, and he was afraid.

He walked on, for he could not think of any other thing to do. At last he came to some rocks which seemed different, three grouped together, huge and dark and leaning a little toward each other. He was grateful for the sight; if he had passed them before he was almost certain he would have remembered them. He went closer and in the dimness the rocks looked menacing and enormous and made him tremble a little. But he forced himself to go in among them and there in the center of the three it was sheltered from the winds and gave some impression of safety and protection. It was chilly but not cold and at last Dilar lay down on the sand and pulled his cape over his head and face and slept.

He woke still tired and sore from his fall, hungry and stiff and terribly thirsty. Once again the darkness had lessened but he did not know whether it was morning, noon, or evening. He stepped out from the circle of rocks and could not remember which way he had come or how he had planned to go on. But he wasted no time thinking of these things. Instead he set out, any way, any road, it did not matter as long as he was moving. He could not bear to think of sitting or standing still in this uncanny place.

His thirst grew worse and worse and his tongue felt like a stick of wood in his mouth. When he tried to swallow, he coughed sharply instead. There must be water somewhere, spring or pool or well, there must be water for he had heard animals and a bird and they must surely have water to live. He almost laughed to think that he, a boy of the Raft People, half fish, his days spent in the water as much as out, should die of thirst.

He walked on. His throat was choked with dryness, he could feel the strange, small winds sucking the juices from him as they blew from every direction. He grew so wretched he forgot to look for springs or pools and simply walked on, staring straight ahead and hardly thinking at all.

So Dilar would have passed the man if the man had not been directly in his way. He was standing, head thrown back, eyes closed, dressed in a dirty, unsewn garment tied at the shoulders and hanging in rags about his knees, his hands raised above his head and his matted hair streaming down his body. He did not turn at Dilar's approach, he did not lower his head or move.

Dilar strained to speak but his throat was closed with thirst. He took a step nearer and put a hand on the man's shoulder.

"Water!" he gasped at last, in a voice cracked and harsh with dryness.

At first the man did not move but then he stepped away from Dilar as though shaking off a vine that had brushed annoyingly against him.

"Water!" croaked Dilar again, and this time the man seemed to have heard. He lowered his head and arms, opened his eyes, and drew from somewhere at his side a sharp stone knife!

CHAPTER 11

Dilar fell to his knees and squeaks and whistles came from his throat. He was somehow not afraid of the man and his knife, he only wanted to explain that he was perishing already so there was no need to stab him. The man walked by him without a look and Dilar turned his head and saw him approach one of the lumpy, thistly plants and cut off the tip of one of the stubby branches. The section was like a small barrel, sealed at both ends, and the man stuck his knife into one end and made an opening and said, "Here, drink," as he held it out.

Dilar seized it and held it to his mouth. The liquid that rushed between his lips was thin, flavorless, not sweet, salty, nor sour, neither hot nor cold. Still it was wet and he drank greedily, turning the strange goblet higher and higher to drain the last drops.

When he was done the man took the piece of plant from him and said in a flat voice, "You have left none for me. Here it is the custom to share the waters of the dobun tree."

"I am s-s-sorry," stammered Dilar, glad to find he had his voice once more. "I didn't know. I was very thirsty, dying of thirst."

The man said nothing more. With his knife he began

89

to pare away the skin with its sharp spines. Dilar looked down at his hands which bled in two or three places from the pricks of the thorns. In his eagerness to drink he had not felt the wounds till now.

When the man had peeled away the rind of the dobun tree he cut off a piece of the flesh and handed it to Dilar. "Eat," he said and cut a piece for himself. Dilar ate. Like the juice the flesh was tasteless, queer and pulpy and tough when he bit into it. Then, seeming to dissolve between his teeth, it slid down his throat almost without his knowing he had swallowed. Still it was food. Dilar ate and watched the man.

If this was all he had to eat no wonder he was so thin, Dilar thought, for the man was no more than bone and leathery brown skin. In his dark, wrinkled face his eyes were huge, light-colored, and blank. Nothing looked out of them, not welcome or fear, not kindness or rejection. *Not*, thought Dilar suddenly. He is not here.

When they had eaten all of the portion of dobun tree, the man stooped and picked up the parings and carried them over to the tree and laid them at its foot. Again he raised his arms over his head and stood with eyes closed and head thrown back. He was still and silent, like a tree himself, for a long time. And then in a faint whisper, no more than the scratching of grains of sand stirred by the wind, he spoke. "As you are a dobun tree, so am I a dobun tree. As you thrive, I thrive."

Then he lowered his head and arms, opened his eyes, and began to walk away. Dilar ran after him. He was terrified of losing sight of the only other human being left in the world. The man did not look at him or speak.

They walked on and on. Although the man did not seem to be hurrying, his long, thin legs carried him swiftly and Dilar lagged behind and then had to scurry to catch up. His muscles were sore and tired and moving was an effort. Besides, the man was dressed in only his thin single garment while Dilar still wore his leggings and shirt and carried his cape.

"Can't we rest?" he asked at last. The man looked around at him. "I am not tired," he answered. "You may rest when you will."

"But if I stop and you go on, I'll be lost again," cried Dilar desperately. "Please don't leave me. I want to go with you."

The man nodded. "Very well," he agreed, seeming neither pleased nor displeased with the idea. He turned aside and led the way a little farther until they came to another group of three rocks such as the one in which Dilar had taken shelter the night before. It pleased Dilar a little to think he had spied out the only way to be shielded from the constant wind and blowing sand. Were these the same three rocks? No, they were taller and leaned closer together. But who could be sure in this place of mysteries and deceptions?

They stepped into the circle of stones and Dilar spread his cape and lay down. The man stood in the center of the place, and once again held his face to the sky and closed his eyes and seemed to go into a kind of sleep or trance. Dilar fell into a drowse, not sleep but almost sleep. All his body and sinews seemed to dissolve into the sand and he himself to float above it. He thought he lay that way a long, long time but he could not be sure. When

91

he opened his eyes, he felt rested and ready to go on and he stood up. The man had disappeared. At length, just as Dilar had decided he had been deserted, the man came from behind one of the rocks and watched while Dilar picked up his possessions and prepared to journey on.

When they left the circle of rocks, the man stopped and turned to face the stones. Dilar waited patiently while the man stood in his queer, silent thanksgiving. At last he said in his strange whisper, "As you are stones, so I am a stone. As you endure, I endure."

They set out once more. By and by Dilar saw in the distance what seemed to be a small mountain, but as they approached he saw that it was rather a much larger circle of stones. The boulders were about twenty-five in number and quite high, set close together. Dilar and the man slipped between two of the largest.

Inside the ring of stones were a few smaller stones, three or four of the odd dobun trees, and a handful of people. They were all like the man who accompanied Dilar, terribly thin, brown, leathery, pale-eyed, tangle-haired. They did not look at the newcomers, but continued as they were, sitting cross-legged on the sand, staring into space.

Dilar and the man of the desert sat too. Since there seemed nothing else to do, Dilar also stared into space. He was troubled and confused, things seemed less and less real with every passing moment, and by and by he fell once again into the strange state of neither sleeping nor waking which had overtaken him when he was resting.

Dimly he was aware that more of the desert people had

92

come into the rock shelter. One of them was standing near him drinking from a dobun tree section. Abruptly the section was held out to Dilar and a voice said, "Drink."

It was a woman's voice, high pitched and even melodious, but containing no more warmth or interest than the man's. Dilar took the drink, for he was thirsty again, and later shared the pulp with her. "Thank you," he said when he was done, and out of her huge, colorless eyes she gazed at him indifferently and then walked over to the dobun tree nearby and repeated the ritual Dilar had seen the man use.

The light faded, but just as it was never really light, now it was not truly dark; just as it was never either quiet or noisy, now it was hushed, with the only sounds the faint grating of sand and wind. Dilar could think of nothing to do but sleep.

In the still dark the man got up and walked away from him and Dilar sensed it at once and roused himself and hurried through the twilight to catch up with him. When he came up with the figure walking ahead of him, for a minute he was not sure this was his rescuer of yesterday.

What difference can it make? he asked himself. These people are all surely just alike, the Not People—that would be a good name for them—and one would serve me as well as another.

Still when he recognized a long, crooked scar down the desert man's leg and knew that this really was the man he had been with before, he felt somehow comforted and reassured.

"Have you a name?" he asked after a while.

"Name? What is a name?" asked the desert man.

"A word that is yours to be called by," explained Dilar. "Just as other people have their own names that are words that they can be called by."

"I would not want to call anyone," answered the man. "No one would want to call me."

"I wanted to call you," pointed out Dilar.

"Why?" asked the man, and Dilar could not reply.

They walked on. The sky grew lighter and suddenly the man stopped and threw back his head, raised his arms, closed his eyes, and stood motionless. Dilar waited beside him. Finally the man spoke his invocation. "As you are light, I am light. As you grow and change and die, I grow and change and die."

Then he threw himself on the ground and lay flat on his face. Dilar waited again, and when the man stood up he heard him whisper. "As you are earth, I am earth. As all things become you and you become all things, so all things become me and I become all things."

He stood up and took two or three quick running steps, moving lightly, and cried in a voice that was almost gay, "Wind! Sand!" and turning quickly in four directions repeated the words and the running steps.

After that he walked steadily on as though he had not paused at all. Dilar followed a few paces behind. These must be the wise men he had heard about, these people who knew how to be content with so little, who wanted and needed next to nothing, who lived at peace with even the sand and wind. These must be the ones who could answer his questions.

For several days Dilar and the desert man wandered over the sand. Sometimes they stopped and the man would sit for long, long periods, either staring straight in front of him or with his face turned up to the clouds, and in those times Dilar dared not speak to him. Instead he himself withdrew into sleep, or rather into that strange drowsing state which seemed always to be waiting for him when he stopped moving about.

It began to seem to Dilar that this was the way all men lived, the way he had always lived, to walk and eat the flesh and drink the juice of the dobun tree and then to sit watching the swirl and swing of the colored mists, in and out and round about, changing and fading and brightening until a sort of swoon overtook the watcher and he sank into nothingness.

He hardly ever thought now about the rafts or his father and grandfather. He never thought about going back to them, nor did he think about going on.

Once as they walked Dilar realized suddenly that he still carried the things Norna had given him, the cape and leggings and cap and even Wingo's bright scarf. Every time they stopped he had without realizing it put his belongings carefully aside and taken them with him when they set out again. He looked at them wonderingly. Should he go on burdening himself with these things?

He turned suddenly to the desert man. "Are you a wise man?" he asked abruptly.

"Wise?" repeated the man. "Who could be wise? There is no wisdom."

"Can you answer my questions?" persisted Dilar.

"All questions are one question," said the man. "All answers are one answer. Wind and sand ask no questions and they receive no answers."

"Am I wind? Am I sand?" asked Dilar wonderingly, and something stirred uneasily behind the desert man's eyes.

"All things are one thing," he said.

"When everything is nothing, all things must be one thing," Dilar said. And then he burst out: "Why are my people on the rafts? Do they go around and around? Where is that Better Place and will they ever reach it?"

The desert man stared at him a long time. "What difference does it make?" he asked. "All places are one place. Wind and sand ask no questions and receive no answers."

They walked on in silence. That night Dilar fell into a deeper sleep than usual and while he slept he had a dream. In his dream he had returned to Norna's house. He saw the green meadow around it and the trees loaded with fruit beside it. He heard Dorna crying out in anger and impatience because the hens had turned over the basket of mushrooms she had left by the doorstep and were now contentedly eating them, and he heard Norna's clear laughter at Dorna's grumbles. He only heard his friends; he did not see them. He was filled with a sudden longing to see Dorna and to walk among the pumpkins.

When he woke, the wind, instead of shifting softly here and there, for the first time since he had been in the wilderness blew steadily from one direction. Sand stung his face and a sudden sharp scent, fresh and biting, filled the air.

The desert man was gone. There was no sign of him anywhere about. Dilar gathered up his cape and his other possessions. He turned his back to the wind and set out across the sand. He knew how to get along, he did not now need the man. No doubt they would meet again in front of some dobun tree or in some ring of stones.

And suddenly Dilar stopped. He stood for a little quite still with the wind blowing strongly and steadily against his back and then he turned about and headed into the wind, walking as fast as he could toward whatever place the wind came from, bearing that pungent smell.

CHAPTER 12

The wind blew harder and the colored haze thinned and streamed away in ragged ribbons. Dilar began to run toward the clearer, brighter air he spied in front of him. The wind tousled his hair around his face and made a deep fluttering sound in his ears. After the strange colors of the desert the countryside into which he was now venturing seemed bleached and pale, with white sand, tan and yellow grasses, and a faded blue sky. Still Dilar thought it enchanting, and he ran on, amazed at how clearly he could see the hillocks of sand ahead of him and how accurately he could judge distances and how steadily the horizon held its place.

Tall plumy grasses grew in patches here and there, and once a rabbit jumped from one patch and scampered to another, startling Dilar so that he dropped his bundle of clothing and had to stop to retrieve it. Birds flew overhead, black and white birds with red bills and gray and white birds with yellow feet, calling to each other in shrill, stuttering voices. Little blue-backed creatures with many legs scuttled sideways in front of him, but he did not pause to look at them. He ran on and on and when at last he reached the dunes and climbed up to the top, there in front of him lay the windy sea.

It was not the first time he had seen the sea. Twice with Dorna he had climbed the mountain behind her house to a point where they could look down on a grape-blue sea, could watch the long creamy-edged wrinkles of the waves creep toward shore, and see the mysterious, deep shadows just below the surface of the water.

But he had not known what the sea was like close at hand. He ran down the sliding, shifting heap of sand and out onto the beach. The green water came toward him, piling up and piling up and piling up until it was too tall to stand any longer but dropped, roaring and tumbling and falling and pounding on top of itself with a thunder that shook the beach and sent the pale froth of its last breath hissing up the sand to die around Dilar's feet. He cried out and ran up and down in excitement, leaping and waving his arms, dizzy with the noise and the fresh, keen smell and the crying birds and the wind.

He ran into the water, splashing and kicking. Some of the spray leaped up into his face; he put out his tongue to lick it away from his lips and was startled at the salt taste of it. It had been so long since he had put into his mouth anything but the flat juice and the dull flesh of the dobun tree that this sharp savor amazed him. He scooped up some water in his hand and sipped it cautiously. Often on the rafts the water had been faintly salty. Those must have been times when they were near the sea and the sea water had somehow got into the river, he told himself. Now the bitter tang reminded him that he was on a journey, looking for something. He waded back to shore and picked up his bundle and stood wondering what to do next.

He would have liked to stay by the sea for a while. It was beautiful; something in him rejoiced at the sight of it and the sound of it. He might live here happily the rest of his life, if he knew how. But he did not know how. He did not even know how to get anything to eat. Here were no fruit trees, no springs, no bulging pantries, not even a dobun tree. There was no sign of another living person— no one to tell him how to live here, certainly no wise man to answer his questions. He must go on.

He set out along the beach, walking on the sand moistened and packed firm by the hammering waves. Occasionally a shell lay in his path and he picked up and examined each one. Once he thought he saw a man ahead of him, but when he came closer he saw that it was a tall, gray bird with a plumed head and long legs. It stood in the shallow waves and watched him as he passed.

There was still no sign of other people. So at length he turned inland and climbed the dunes again. After an hour's walk he came to a scrubby woodland and then some fields with a faint path running across them. He followed the path and it grew wider and more worn until it was almost a road. There were wooden fences along the way such as Norna's people used sometimes to confine ewes and lambs, to keep them from wandering up the mountain. But no animals grazed inside these fences. Instead young green things grew there in odd straight rows.

Dilar was puzzled. Someone had put the plants there that way; it was not natural for beans to grow in long lines. But why? And why fence them in? Surely beans did not get up and run up the hillsides? Or did they? He leaned over the fence and looked at them uneasily but they seemed to be fastened firmly in the earth, as most plants were.

He came to more woodland. This land, Dilar saw, was not like the land where the People Against the Tigers lived. The hillsides were steep and the soil thin and rocky, the trees scraggly and small and crooked. Here was no lush meadowland, no riot of bushes and vines bearing fruits and vegetables, no meal of mushrooms, nuts, or berries always by the roadside.

Still it was a beautiful place in its own way. New greenery hung like lace over the scrawny trees and scattered brush, sometimes tinged with red or gold or pink. Patches of tiny yellow and blue flowers grew among the rocks. They seemed to Dilar lovelier and more fragile for growing so bravely out of that poor earth, surrounded by dead leaves and bits of rocks and broken twigs. He stopped and got down on his knees to see the bright gold star in the center of the soft petals.

The road wound uphill and then down. Dilar came on springs and drank the sweet, fresh water. He was getting very hungry but there was nothing to eat. By and by he came on more fences confining their lines of green growing things and in one of those pens a man was working, chopping away at the earth with a long-handled tool. Though Dilar walked by slowly the man did not look up. He passed a house and then another house, with a woman washing clothes in a pot in front of it. She saw him and nodded, and he waved back. He wanted very much to ask her for something to eat, but he was afraid. He had never done such a thing and did not really know how to go about it. The sun shone directly overhead. He passed more fields, more houses, and several people who stared curiously at him or smiled but did not speak.

At last he came on a man sitting by the roadside eating bread and cheese out of a leather sack. Dilar stopped and waited and the man grinned and held out some of the bread and a piece of cheese. "Here," he said. "You look hungry. You're welcome to share what I've got."

Dilar took the food gratefully and stuffed some of the bread into his mouth. He was so hungry he almost choked swallowing the bread and hardly noticed how it tasted, though it had been so long since he had eaten anything but the flavorless meat of the dobun tree.

"You're a stranger," asserted the man, and Dilar could only nod.

The man nodded back and then he said, "If you're seeking your fortune, you've come to the wrong place. Hard work's the only fortune you'll get around here, for there are no riches." Then he laughed. "Ah, but what am I saying? We've enough to eat and some to share with a stranger. That's ample riches."

Dilar chewed and swallowed and then he said, "I have not come to seek a fortune. I have come to find the answers to some questions."

The man took the last piece of cheese from his sack, broke it in two, and gave half to Dilar. Then he folded the sack and stuck it inside his shirt. "I hope you find them," he told Dilar. "A question can be as bothersome as a biting fly on a summer's afternoon. But sometimes the answers can be bothersome too. Good luck to you, and now I must go back to work." He climbed over

102

the fence and plodded off between the rows of new plants.

"Thank you for the food," called Dilar, and the man raised a hand in acknowledgment but did not turn around.

Dilar had traveled a space farther when the road branched for the first time since he had set foot upon it. One road ran downhill past more fences and farms, and the other, not so well marked, ran steeply up. Dilar hesitated. He should go toward the houses and people, he knew. But the sun was hot and the uphill road twisted among trees and gray rocks and seemed somehow more adventurous and inviting. He turned that way and began to climb.

He was hardly out of sight of the crossroads before he regretted his choice. The path was steep and difficult to climb. There might not be anyone at all along this road to offer him food and a night's lodging.

But then he consoled himself: since he had no idea where he was going, nor much more of an idea why, it hardly mattered which way he took.

The trace had leveled out, was no longer climbing. The sun would set shortly. Dilar looked about, wondering if these woods offered any sort of shelter. There were no habitations as far as he could see, no paths other than the one he walked, no fences, no cleared places planted with rows of young potatoes. Ah, well, if he had to sleep on the ground with his cape for cover—he was well used to it. And even on the mountains among the tigers he had not been harmed.

Still there was some daylight and he trudged on, hoping for a place that suited him more than these open woods. And then he saw a light through the trees, the blaze of a small fire. He left the path and walked toward the light cautiously, and at last he could make out a man's figure hunched on a log by the flames.

Dilar stood hesitating. The man simply sat. Across the fire from him several animals moved about, and beyond was a dark shape Dilar took to be a house.

Suddenly the man called out impatiently, "Come on, come on. Sit down, sit down. Don't stand there in the dark! Come on."

At first Dilar thought he was addressing one of the animals and then the man turned his head and called again, "Come and sit down!"

Slowly Dilar approached the fire. Once again the man was looking away from him but he patted the log beside him meaning for Dilar to sit, and then he said, "It will be ready soon."

Dilar waited a moment and then he asked timidly, "What will be ready?"

"The soup, the soup!" cried the man irritably. "The *soup* will be ready!"

"Oh," said Dilar. There was a pot on a trivet in the fire. That must be the soup. He stared at it hungrily and then he turned his eyes to the man who sat beside him.

The man was old, not so old as Grandfather, but older perhaps than Dilar's father, Gimal, older than Wingo. He was rather dirty and scruffy looking, an ugly man with a twisted nose and a scraggly beard and a scar over one eyebrow.

The man turned his head and stared at Dilar and Dilar

looked quickly away. Embarrassed, he asked, "Are those antelopes?" nodding at the little horned beasts who chewed away at the bushes.

"Goats, goats," answered the man brusquely. "Only goats. Stupid creatures." The goats rolled their wicked yellow eyes at one another and grinned gently.

Suddenly the man stood up and walked to the door of the hut. He went in and in a few minutes came out with two bowls and a loaf of dark bread. He filled the bowls from the pot and handed one to Dilar.

The soup was not rich and thick and flavorful, like Wingo's soup, but it was hot and filling and with the bread made a good meal. When Dilar had eaten, he set his bowl on the ground, spoke his thanks for the supper, and stood up to be on his way.

"Sit down, sit down," bade the man again crossly. "Now it's dark, where would you be going this time of night? Sit down and be quiet and when he comes we'll go to bed."

"When who comes?" asked Dilar, still standing, for he did not like being ordered about so much.

"My niddy goat, my niddy goat," said the man. "Out there in the woods, no doubt, if some wolf hasn't eaten him. That's what he wants me to think, you know, that he's been eaten by a wolf. He thinks I'll cry and be sorry and then he can come running up laughing his silly head off." The man spat into the fire. "Some day a wolf really will eat him, and then he'll rue the day." He leaned toward Dilar and whispered, "He's listening, you know, out there in the brush. I can see his white spots." And he grinned, looking a lot like the goats himself.

"My name is Vigan," he said suddenly. "I have lived here, off and on, for the life spans of three niddy goats and four years of this one."

"I am Dilar " said Dilar. He frowned. "I do not know how long I have lived anywhere."

The man laughed. "Not long. I can tell that." There was a rustling in the bushes behind him and he smiled a smile of real affection. "Here comes my niddy goat," he said softly.

The goat strolled past the fire and toward the hut. It walked proudly and very daintily on small hoofed feet, but its horns and beard were fierce. Dilar thought it would take a great wolf to kill and eat such a one.

"Argh!" cried the man. "Fool goat!" He sprang to his feet and herded the other goats together and drove them all into a little fenced place behind his house and barred the gate.

"Now come along, come along," he urged Dilar. "It's past my bedtime."

It was dark in the little hut. Coals glowed on the hearth but Vigan lit no candle and did not even stir up the fire. He spread a blanket on the floor and urged Dilar to lie down. Lying there Dilar watched the coals wink out, heard the old man climb into bed, listened to the goats stamping their feet and the sound of a night bird.

He closed his eyes for a second and when he opened them again it was morning. Faint daylight came through the open door and the one window, and he could see Vigan kneeling by the hearth, rekindling the fire.

He fed it and blew on it and coaxed it and suddenly flames shot up and made a bright light in the small room.

106

Vigan turned and looked down at the boy on his pallet and caught his breath in surprise. "Why, you're one of them!" he exclaimed. "One of them! There hasn't been one of them this way in thirty years!"

CHAPTER 13

"What do you mean—*them?*" asked Dilar in a whisper. "Who are—*them?*"

"The Raft People," answered Vigan briskly. "The Raft People, of course. You are one of them, aren't you?"

"How did you know?" cried Dilar. "How did you know? What do you know about my people?"

"Enough and too much," said the man briefly. "I've left you some food. Eat. I must tend my goats. They long to be out looking for wolves."

"Wait, wait," Dilar begged, but the man went out as though he hadn't heard. Dilar sprang up from his pallet and went to follow, but then he decided that perhaps he should eat. The day portended a great deal. He might be traveling again in an hour. He would eat.

The food was a kind of boiled grain, sweetened with honey, and a bowl of goat's milk. Dilar had grown accustomed to different kinds of foods, no matter how odd tasting, so it was excitement, not flavor, that made it almost impossible for him to swallow the mush and gulp down the milk. But he forced himself to eat it all. He glanced around the hut—a single room and a lean-to, rather like Norna's, but not so light and airy, and nowhere near so clean and tidy. Everything was dusty and all of a heap and scattered about.

When he was finished with his meal Dilar picked up his bundle and went outside. Vigan was shutting the gate to the pen with one hand and holding the niddy goat firmly by one horn with the other. The rest of the herd stood about looking wicked. Dilar went to help. "Are you a wise man?" he asked as Vigan shoved the bar in place.

"All men are wise about one thing or another," answered Vigan. "I am wise about goats. Especially niddy goats." And he began to walk off through the trees still holding the niddy goat's horn. The others fell in behind.

Dilar ran after them. They walked till they came to a path that led upward, and presently they left the woods behind and came to a sort of scrubby meadowland. Dilar could bear the silence no longer. "Are you a wise man?" he persisted.

Vigan chewed a weedstalk for a minute before he said, "If you mean am I an old man who has learned a lot and thought about it some, yes, I am. If you mean can I tell you what to do and how to do it, yes, I may be. If you mean can I tell you whether to do it and why you should or shouldn't, no, I'm not. Oh, I might know, but only a fool tries to answer such questions for another. Wisdom is like water: there comes a point where it runs into the ground and if you want it you must dig it out yourself."

He chewed some more and then added thoughtfully, "Of course, I might tell you why. I might tell you lots of things if there was a good enough reason."

Dilar frowned. What to do and how to do it would be all he wanted to know. They walked on until they came to a spot where the grass grew less sparsely and the bushes and rocks were more scattered. Here Vigan stopped and the niddy goat broke away from him and raced away down the slope. "I have my eye on you," Vigan bawled after it. "I know what you're up to, every minute. You and your tricks!" He spat into the bushes, sat down on a rock, and said morosely, "He'll be away again. I'm lying when I say I know what he's up to. Some wolf will eat him yet."

Dilar was impatient with the niddy goat. "Tell me about the Raft People," he begged.

"*You* tell *me*," returned Vigan. "If anybody should know about the Raft People, it's you."

And that was strange, Dilar thought. He should know. And yet he didn't. There had been a time when the rafts were all his world, and he had gone from one end of the flotilla to the other a thousand times in his life. Only now that he had left it behind had he discovered that he knew nothing about it.

"Why are the rafts in that tunnel?" he insisted. "Do they go around and around? Is there a Better Place? Tell me. I know you know. You must know. You knew I was one of them. You said there had been others of my people who came this way."

"So I did," admitted Vigan. "And so there have been." He sat pondering, staring up at the craggy mountainside. Two great birds soared along the cliffsides swaying and dipping as they rode the rising current of the bright morning air.

"Do you see those eagles?" Vigan asked suddenly. "They have a nest on that cliff. At noon the hen will lay an egg in her nest. If you can climb up there and fetch that egg back unbroken, you will learn something about your people."

"How?" cried Dilar. "How will I learn? Is there something in the egg? Is it magic? Is there an enchantment on my people? Must I be the one to free them?"

"Ask me no questions," Vigan replied. "Fetch the egg. That's all I can tell you."

Dilar sprang up from the rock. "Take your things," said Vigan crossly. "If you fall off the mountainside and get killed I don't want to have to bother with your bundle." He held it out.

Dilar took it from him. "How do I get there?" he asked. Vigan pointed. "Take that path. It will lead you to the bottom of the cliff. From there you must find your own way up."

Dilar was angry with the man for his brusque ways. He set out toward the path carrying his bundle. "If there are more eggs than one in the nest," Vigan called after him, "put your hand on them and take the warmest. That will be freshest. You have to have the freshest one."

"Very well," Dilar shouted, without looking around. He hoped the niddy goat would run away.

Soon he came to a dense evergreen woods. Birds flashed and sang among the branches and the sun called forth the spicy scent of the trees. Strange pale flowers bloomed among the fallen needles. In spite of being so troubled and so avid to find the eagle's egg, Dilar stopped and drew a deep breath of the fragrant air, listened to the voices of the birds, and stooped to examine the little nodding flowers. All his years in the darkness of the tunnel, when he had not even known that such things as this existed, came into his mind. Gimal and Bimar and Grandfather and the others were still there, still not knowing how beautiful and astonishing the world outside the river was, how it could delight the eyes and fill the heart with wonder.

He trembled a little thinking how he had been chosen to break the spell and bring them out into the light of day. It was an awesome thing to be given such a task to perform. He could not imagine why it had fallen to him to do this thing, to him, Dilar of the Raft People, who was not stronger or braver or better or wiser than any other.

But he had been chosen. Now he knew. Vigan had told him so, and in his heart he found it to be true, that he must discover the truth and try to do what was required of him.

The path climbed and climbed through the woods and beyond. And when at last it ended Dilar saw that his task was going to be indeed a hard one. His heart quailed, looking up at the tall cliffs, and he wondered for a minute if climbing to the eagle's nest would not be impossible. He had thought that going up would be rather like ascending the Mountains of the Tigers to Wingo's cave. He had not known it would mean going straight up this bare rock wall.

He sat down and scanned the precipice. After a bit he saw that there were handholds and toeholds, cracks and crevices, roots and branches, all the way to the top. It would not be easy, it would be difficult and dangerous. He might very well fall and be killed. But if there was nothing else to be done, there was nothing else to be done. He must try, and that was that.

He opened his bundle and took out the leggings and

put them on, to protect himself from bruises and scratches. He put his cap on his head and tied the scarf around his waist, tucking the ends in securely so that they would not catch on branches or outcroppings. His cape he left lying on the ground. If he fell perhaps someone would find it and make use of it. Norna would like to think it went on being of service to someone in need.

Then he turned to the cliff. He walked along the foot of it and nearly gave up hope of even starting, for though there was a wide ledge only a little over his head, he found no way to climb up to it. At length he came on two stones, tumbled from somewhere above, and lying one on top of the other, making a kind of a step for him. He found a handhold and struggled and fought and pulled himself up.

For a while after that it was fairly easy, only a matter of deciding which places were safest to put his hands and feet and which would most easily lead to the next series of holds. He did not look down for he was afraid he would be discouraged by his progress. Only when he came to a shelf wide enough to crouch on and get his breath for a bit did he glance back at the way he had come. He gasped and put his hands over his eyes and clung to the ledge and resolved not to look again.

Toward the top it was much harder, the rocks were worn, apt to give and crumble under his weight. But he was almost there. Two more upward steps and he would be able to see over the very top. He reached up, testing the cracks, and then he heard a rushing noise, a strange loud whirring-booming sound over his head. He glanced up and saw the eagle descending toward him and he thought he had never seen anything so huge as those wings spread across the sky nor anything so savage as those reaching talons. He thought this quite clearly and calmly, but even as he thought it he realized from some stony core of his being that he was the eagle's victim, that those vast beating wings and those great grasping claws were for Dilar of the Raft People and that they might be the last things he would ever see.

He clawed frantically at the wall and squeezed himself flat, flat against it. The eagle rushed on at him, it screamed a shrill, terrible scream of elation; he felt it strike his head and almost fainted with shock and fear. His skull had been split open, he would fall, he would die! Dizzy, panting, with the light growing dim he still clung grimly to the wall and the eagle plunged down, down, uttering its high-pitched, cruel cries.

It took only a second for Dilar to understand. The cool air on his head helped revive him and, feeling it, he knew what had happened. The cap! Norna's heavy cap of hide and fur had saved him! He was unhurt, and what the eagle carried with him so triumphantly was only a cap, not the whole back of Dilar's head, as he—and the eagle —had for a stricken moment thought.

He could not remember afterward how he got to the top. He went up so quickly, clawing at the rock in such panic that he supposed he must have gone up as a fly climbs, clinging to bare surfaces with fingers made adhesive by terror and haste. There at the top were rocks and bushes and he dived in among them, crouching between two big stones while the eagles swooped down at him again and again, for now both birds had come to do battle.

So he was here. But what good had it done him to get here? He dared not go near the eagles' nest. If he should by some miracle get to the nest and manage to take the egg away, he would never be able to get back down the cliff with it. They would tear him to pieces. He could wait till nightfall, but trying to descend that sheer wall in the dark would be his death, he was certain.

Ah, Vigan had tricked him. He had meant for Dilar to be killed. Whatever the secret of the Raft People, it was something he was not destined to learn now or ever. He gritted his teeth in rage and the monstrous birds screeched and snatched.

After a while the birds went away. He no longer heard their ear-piercing shrieks nor the booming noise of their descending wings. He raised his head cautiously and they were on him again in a moment, screaming, grabbing, beating the air, thundering down on him. He struck his head on one of the protective stones as he hurled himself between them. It hurt sharply and a little blood trickled down his face. He was once again filled with anger at Vigan and then remembered suddenly that if he had never stepped off the raft this would never have happened. People who did foolish things must expect to die of their foolishness.

The eagles' cries faded. Dilar turned his head and peered up cautiously. The two big birds were circling higher and higher above him in the cloudy sky. He knew their savage eyes were fixed on him still, that if he showed so much as an ear tip in seconds they would dive down, ripping and tearing.

And then something happened. One of the eagles called with a new urgency, and the birds ceased their circling and flew out of the range of his vision. And then both screamed together, setting the rocks quivering with echoes, and their voices came toward him and then fell below the cliff edge. He sprang out of his hiding place for immediately he knew what had happened: the eagles had spied some other victim on the cliffside and were switching their attack.

He looked around swiftly and found the nest, a great bundle of dry twigs and sticks, wide enough to hold a sheep, it seemed to him. He ran as he had never run before and saw the two white eggs, bigger than his fist, lying there, and put his hand over each one and took the warmer. Oh, he would show Vigan; he would get back alive and with the egg and then the old goat man would be the one who had been tricked, not Dilar.

Holding the egg between his cupped hands he ran. But in his haste and triumph and excitement he did not run back the way he had come; he ran in the opposite direction, for it was less obstructed by undergrowth and rocks. And then he realized that this way offered him no cover, no place to hide. The eagles would be back any minute now and they would know he had taken the precious egg!

CHAPTER 14

He ran on, for he was too afraid to go back. He was afraid, too, to turn away from the edge of the mountain onto the open tableland that capped its height. But he must find shelter, quickly, quickly. Along here the cliff was covered with vines that sprawled over the stony brink and hung below the rim. They caught at his feet and he ran to the edge and looked over. He would jump down onto the next ledge and there he could take refuge behind the curtain of half-leafed vines.

He did not stop to think; he knew he would not have the courage if he stopped to think. He leaped, cradling the egg against him. His feet struck the shelf and he teetered over the edge and almost dropped the egg, and then with one hand managed to grab the vines and save himself. His heart beat achingly in his chest and he was half suffocated with fear. He sank to his knees.

He pushed backward among the vines and they closed around him. He was safe for the moment. The eagles could not find him here. He sat trembling and shaking until his breath came more easily and he was certain that he was still alive. The past hour seemed as terrible and unreal and impossible as a nightmare, and he was not at all sure that he had not after all fallen from the cliff when the eagle had first attacked.

And then pride and delight in what he had done surged over him, and he pictured in his mind's eye Vigan's shame and abashment when he handed him the egg. He must, of course, get the egg safely down the rest of the way, but he believed he could do it. He had done so much, he could do the rest.

He untied the scarf from around his waist and knotted the egg into one end of it. He looped it around his neck so that the egg lay between his shoulder blades. This would leave his hands free, and since he would be facing the cliff as he climbed down, the fragile shell would not be in danger of being crushed.

He parted the vines and looked out. The eagles were nowhere in sight. The cliff below him looked somehow less perilous and steep than he had imagined possible. Perhaps it was, for he went down easily and quickly and though he had to hang by his hands and drop the last few feet, where the wall was smooth and without handholds, it was not far and he kept his feet and only jarred his teeth and cracked his shins a little.

He searched for the path, eager to get away from the eagles and back to Vigan. He found his cape that he had left lying at the foot of the cliff and it was torn to ribbons. It must have been this that the eagles had spied, the thing that had drawn them from their attack on him. They must have thought it was a person lying on the ground. Once again Norna's clothes had saved his life.

The sun was going down and shadows growing long when he got back to the meadow. Vigan had built a fire. While he was still a good way off, Dilar could see him bending over it. The goats were gathered nearby. There was suddenly about Vigan an air of mystery and strangeness.

"Ah, he is the wise man," thought Dilar. "I have been chosen then, and the egg will tell me what the magic is. It is like the stories. I have been given a task and I have done it, in spite of danger and hardship, and now I will have passed the test and I will know the answers."

He carried the precious egg carefully the rest of the way. When he came up to Vigan, the man turned and said, "Ah, you've done it, Dilar of the Raft People, I congratulate you. It can't have been easy."

Silently Dilar held out the egg. The man took it with a cry of joy and popped it into a little kettle of boiling water on the fire and watched it eagerly.

"Will you say a charm?" asked Dilar softly after a minute. "Do you need magic herbs or spices?"

"Whatever for?" asked Vigan. "A really fresh eagle's egg needs only a little salt and I have that. Butter, now, that would be better, but not goat butter. I can't stand that."

Dilar stared in disbelief. Was the wise man going to eat the eagle's egg? Was this what Dilar had risked his life for? He watched as Vigan carefully poured the water from the kettle, cracked the steaming egg, and scooped out the contents into a bowl. "Oh, I can't remember *when* I've had a fresh eagle's egg. Here, hand me that cup and I'll share it with you."

"You only wanted that egg to eat!" shouted Dilar. "You tricked me! You cheated me! You said I would learn something about the Raft People from that egg."

"No, I did not say that," interrupted Vigan. "I said,

if you fetch back the egg you would learn something of your people. And so you will, for I will tell you. As for fetching the egg, you needn't have done it if you thought it was too dangerous or difficult. I could have done without. But you are young and strong, and to do a difficult and dangerous thing ought to give you pleasure. It's the reason for being young and strong."

He ate, scraping up the last bit of egg and wiping out the bowl with bread. "I am old and weak. To do a deed of daring I have to rely on younger bodies and hearts." He cackled with sudden laughter. "I can't even keep up with my niddy goat. He's gone again. Better eat your egg while it's still hot. It's good."

Sullenly Dilar took his bowl and ate. The egg was delicious; Vigan was right. But he should not have deceived Dilar. *I would not have climbed that cliff and come so close to death for a meal, no matter how savory,* he thought.

But he had done it, for he was young and strong and brave, as Vigan had said. Once again he felt proud and sure of himself.

"I would have brought you the egg if you had asked," he said. "You needn't have tricked me."

"Oh, would you have?" asked Vigan and gave him a strange look. Dilar was shamed, having just thought that indeed he wouldn't have. He was afraid that Vigan knew his thoughts.

"Perhaps you would. And then perhaps you wouldn't. Anyway I like playing tricks on people. I have a wicked nature," Vigan said with a grin. "I caught it from the goats."

Dilar could think of nothing to say in answer to this. By and by the niddy goat came wandering up and Vigan said, "Come along then. It'll soon be dark."

Dilar went with him and the goats. He did not want to stay with the man any longer, but he had no choice. The night would be cold and he had lost his hat and cape, he had no food, and he was a long way from any other place where he might lodge. But he would leave as soon as daylight came. He wouldn't stay with Vigan any longer than he had to.

In the morning when he woke on his pallet Vigan was sitting by the fire. He held out to Dilar an old, worn wool coat and then a bowl of mush. "Long ago, before your grandfather's grandfather was born," he said abruptly, "the Raft People lived along the sea. They were fisher-folk and knew all about boats and nets and tides and waves. The winters are hard in this country and they are hardest along the seacoasts, for there the storms are fiercer and the winds blow keener and fishing is out of the question. Sometimes the people starved and some-times the tempests wrecked boats and houses. It was a difficult life.

"Now the fishermen knew about the underground river that ran beneath the mountains and coiled back upon itself and made a great slow circle through caves and tun-nels. During the storms of winter they occasionally fished on that river, for it was full, oh, full of fish. But getting in and out of the entrance was hardly ever possible be-cause of snow and ice and high winds and tides.

"And then there was a particularly savage season and many of the people died, and some niddy goat among them said, 'Let us build rafts and go and live on the underground river, where there are always fish, where storms and winter never come, where we will never be in danger again.' And so they did. All the people went in the entrance and began to go around and around and around and around, endlessly, in the rock tunnels.

"Who knows what happened? Perhaps they forgot where the entrance was. Or perhaps the earth moved and closed it up. Or perhaps they simply did not care any longer to admit to themselves how foolish they had been. At any rate they started telling themselves that they were headed for some Better Place to live and work, that the tunnel did not swallow its own tail, but led them toward some marvelous goal. And now most of them believe this to be the truth and those who do not believe it are ashamed to say so."

He was silent and Dilar stared into the fire.

"Thank you," he said at last.

Vigan shrugged. "It was payment for the egg," he answered.

"But how can I get back in?" Dilar asked. "How can I go back into the tunnel if I cannot find the way in?"

"Why would you want to go back in?" Vigan was astonished.

"I want to bring my people out into the world again!" cried Dilar impatiently. "I want to show them how stupid they have been."

"Why," exclaimed Vigan in disgust, "you haven't learned a thing, have you? Not one thing from all that's happened to you. You might as well have stayed in the tunnel."

"How could I learn anything?" cried Dilar. "I met no wise man on my journey, not one person who could answer my questions or tell me anything about my people."

"All those people told you many things if you had had the wit to listen," said Vigan angrily. "All men are wise about one thing or another—and all men are stupid about an equal number of things. Look at those grasshoppers who call themselves the People Against the Tigers. Oh, they're wise enough. They lead pleasant, happy lives— until something comes along that requires a little fore-thought and preparation. And then they are no use to themselves or anybody else. Look at those creatures in the desert who have arranged to avoid trouble by dying before they are born. Look at your fat friend on the moun-taintop whose nature is so tender he can't bear to notice how cruel he is being."

"How did you know?" Dilar's eyes grew wide. "How did you know I had been with those people? How do you know all about me and where I have been?"

"You bear their marks," Vigan told him. "And you will forever. Don't ask me how I can read the marks, for I won't tell you. It is the privilege of the old and wise to say that age and wisdom account for their knowledge, and let it go at that." He grinned. "It isn't true, but I can't be bothered telling you the truth. It's too hard to believe."

"I would believe you," argued Dilar.

"Oh, ho, you think a lot of yourself, don't you?" ex-claimed Vigan. "You wouldn't, you know. Nothing is harder to believe than the truth. If it weren't so, all men would be good and kind and wise and happy."

Dilar sat for a while in sulky silence. Finally he burst out, "If you are so wise and know all about me and can tell me what to do, why can't you help those others? Why can't you tell them what to do?"

"Why should I?" answered Vigan. "They are not cruel or unjust or oppressive to anyone. They are only a little stupid, as all men are a little stupid. They haven't come asking me for help and likely never will. Besides, do you really think anyone could persuade those people to change their ways?" He touched the scar on his forehead lightly. "I'll tell you now that there are few persons who take kindly to having it pointed out to them that they are stupid. It's one of many things they don't like being told."

Dilar thought about that. "I suppose not," he admitted.

"Anyway," went on Vigan and he looked suddenly a little sad, "all things change, in time. Somewhere along the years perhaps the People Against the Tigers will give up their lazy ways and start storing food and firewood for winter, and then life may not be so pleasant and gay there. Everybody will start remembering which donkey is his donkey and how many sheep he has and that he is entitled to more pumpkins than his neighbor, and there will be quarrels over sledges and some will start claiming some grapevines for their own, forgetting there are more than enough grapes to go around. I will be sorry to see them become wise in such a stupid way."

"But *my* people haven't time to change," wailed Dilar. "They are dying now. I must bring them out of the tunnel."

"It is the fate of men to die," said Vigan. "You must have better reasons than that."

"I want to bring my grandfather out," said Dilar firmly,

"so that he can see a better place and so that he can see day and the color green."

"Your grandfather!" said Vigan in disgust. "He may be dead by now—or blind. If you brought him out and he lived another fifty years and kept the keenest sight, he would never see those places I have heard of, where snow lies deep on the ground every day of the year and the sun shines at midnight and all the animals go clad in white fur. Or the great hot jungles where there are beasts with teeth longer than you are high. There are things all men must do without seeing and knowing, no matter how far and wide they travel. You must have better reasons."

"I want to bring them out because. . . ." Dilar began and could not think why. Vigan might be right. It would be an arduous journey back to the river, a journey beset with perils and likely ending in failure, for perhaps he could persuade none of them, not Grandfather, not Gimal, nor even Bimar, to leave the shadows for the marvels of space and brightness and the transparent air.

Yet he, Dilar, could try it. He was young and strong. "To do a difficult and dangerous thing is the reason for being young and strong," Vigan had said. At length he repeated stubbornly, "Because."

Vigan jumped to his feet and clapped his hands together. "Ah, now, there's a reason, and you have my blessing. I will help you in what small way I can. Here, take the coat, and I'll give you some food and you can set out."

Dilar was a little taken aback. All at once he was not so eager to start on this journey as he had thought he would be. "I could stay awhile," he protested.

Vigan shrugged. "Very well," he said. "Stay. I would

have thought if the doing was important to you, you would want to leave at once."

"I suppose that is so," answered Dilar.

Vigan filled a leather pouch with bread and cheese. And then he took a piece of goatskin and dipped a twig in some sort of dye and drew a map of all the mountains and how the river ran under them and twisted back to the sea.

"Here," Vigan pointed out, "you must have come out here. The journey around the river takes a year, or nearly so. Soon they will be back at the point where you left them. If you hurry you can be there by that time. See, I have shown you how to avoid the desert, but you yourself must figure out how to elude Wingo and his oatcakes."

"But I have looked over that mountainside," Dilar said. "I cannot find the place I came out. I have searched and searched."

Vigan said, "Search higher. People who go up a mountain to a spot they have come down from seldom go high enough. They misjudge. Coming down is easier than going up."

Now that was one thing Dilar had learned for himself. So perhaps he could find his way into the mountain sooner or later.

A sudden suspicion crossed his mind. "How do I know you are not lying to me?" he asked. "How do I know you are not tricking me again?"

"You don't," answered Vigan indifferently. "You must discover for yourself. But one thing I will tell you: I never lie. I may be wicked but I do not lie. The things I tell you are the truth and it is you who may tell yourself lies. It is the easiest kind of lying done."

"I won't," asserted Dilar.

Vigan sneered. "You think a lot of yourself," he repeated.

Dilar wanted to throw down the coat and pouch and stalk away and leave the goat man. But he needed these things. For Grandfather's sake he swallowed his pride. He turned on his heel and began to walk away.

"Wait, wait," called Vigan. And Dilar halted, for he thought perhaps Vigan was going to tell him something important, or give him some magic thing to help him on his way.

The man walked toward him and when he came up to Dilar he smiled suddenly and Dilar saw for the first time that his eyes were very blue and gentle, that in spite of his ugliness and the scar and the twisted nose he had a kind face.

"Good-by, Dilar," he said. "I wish you luck. No matter what I've said, it is a fine thing to want to show other people the light of day and the loveliness of green growing things. If I had a grandson, it would please me that he would want to do such a thing for me. If you are ever past this way again, come and visit. The niddy goat and I will be glad to see you."

He held out his hand and slowly Dilar put his own into it. "Good-by, Vigan," he answered. "If I am ever by this way again, I'll come to see you."

And then he began to walk swiftly back the way he had come.

About the Author

MARY Q. STEELE was born in Tennessee and has lived there all her life. She began to write shortly after her three children started school. Using the pseudonym Wilson Gage as well as her own name, Mrs. Steele soon was recognized as a leading writer of books for young people.

Mary Steele lives with her husband, William Steele, who is also a writer, in Signal Mountain, Tennessee. She is a self-trained naturalist who enjoys bird-watching and long country walks.

About her writing, Mary Q. Steele says: "I write for whoever will listen. What I am talking about always is the world around us, about stars and mushrooms and foxes and birds and ants and trees. How can I convey to anyone else the magic and the marvel of it, the vast astonishment of being alive? I'm not sure I can, but I intend to go on trying."